Whistling Death

A Marine World Cozy Mystery

Peyton Stone

Authors Writes, LLC

Copyright © 2023 by Authors Writes, Peyton Stone

All rights reserved.

No portion of this book may be reproduced in any form or by any electronic or mechanical means; including information storage and retrieval systems without written permission from the author, except for the use of brief descriptions/quotations in a book review.

Cover design by Getcovers.com

Contents

1. Chapter One — 1
2. Chapter Two — 8
3. Chapter Three — 17
4. Chapter Four — 27
5. Chapter Five — 37
6. Chapter Six — 49
7. Chapter Seven — 61
8. Chapter Eight — 67
9. Chapter Nine — 78
10. Chapter Ten — 88
11. Chapter Eleven — 97
12. Chapter Twelve — 109
13. Chapter Thirteen — 117

14.	Chapter Fourteen	125
15.	Chapter Fifteen	133
Don't be shy...		140

One

Chapter One

The bottlenose dolphin arced through the air, a shower of salt water falling behind her. She chattered excitedly as she soared majestically through the large hoop KK was holding.

"As you can see, ladies and gentlemen," KK's mother, Katerina, said into the mic. "Majestique is a bit of a showoff."

Majestique, as if in response to the statement, hopped backward, letting her tail propel her as she moved backward in the water. The dolphin backflipped, her tail slapping the water as she dived, spraying some of the kids in the front row, all of whom screamed and laughed. KK grinned, wiping some of the water that had splashed her from her perch over the tank off her face.

"But that doesn't mean Simon doesn't love the spotlight, also," KK's mom added, as Majestique and a male dolphin jumped out of the water and twisted through the air like synchronized divers.

The audience cheered loudly as the two bottlenose dolphins jumped and danced around the tank while KK and her father directed them to jump, flip, talk, dive, and do all kinds of other tricks. KK tossed a ball into the tank, and Majestique grabbed it in her mouth, before bouncing it several times off her nose, one time throwing it so high in the air that she was able to leap from the water and grab it in her mouth before finishing her flip.

KK's father, Joseph, down on the rocks that wrapped around the far end of the tank, threw Simon and Majestique fish as he directed them to leap and swim gracefully into the water, where the audience could watch them through large glass panels. At one point, Simon swam so quickly past the glass that the water flew over the side, splashing the first three rows. Kids and adults alike laughed and clapped. The two dolphins, adoring the attention their tricks were getting them, chattered excitedly, slapping their tails hard against the water to splash more of the onlookers.

For the final trick, Majestique and Simon leaped over the perch KK was standing on, both leaping through hoops in perfect time with one another. Not once or twice, but five times.

"Thank you, guys, very much for coming to Simon and Majestique's last show," Katerina concluded as the dolphins receded into the water for the final time and the audience's applause had died down some. "They've been like family and we know how much they love you, but it's time for them to be released in a couple of days. Thank you for coming and helping their last show be so magical."

Saltwater misted across KK's face as she leaned over the side of the boat, looking ahead into the empty expanse ahead of them.

"I think we'll probably be good here," Katerina noted from the wheel. A moment later, the boat's motor whirred down before going silent entirely. KK dropped the anchor as her mother called to her, "Go help your father with Majestique and Simon, otherwise he'll throw out his back out of pure stubbornness."

The wind whipped her words away but KK could still make it out. She walked to the back of the boat where the sling held the two dolphins. Her father stood there, watching the two mammals, his salt-and-pepper hair slick with salt water.

"Now the best way to release them is—"

"I know, Dad," she acknowledged patiently, smirking slightly. "I've done this a few times now, you know."

"I know," he said, smiling, hazel eyes glinting in the light from the sunset. "But I wouldn't be your father if I wasn't peppering you with advice until I turned blue in the face."

KK rolled her eyes fondly, unable to hold back the smile. That was her dad to a 'T.'

"Why do I feel like you're going to be coming to the aquarium every day even when you say you're retiring?" she teased.

The grin grew wider and he gave her a wink but said nothing. She sighed.

"You know I thought the whole point of you two giving me the business, was for you guys to relax," she stated. "I don't think you giving me business advice twenty-four-seven counts as relaxing."

"I don't know what you're talking about," Joseph replied. "I'm not giving you business advice."

She sighed again, this time accompanying the motion with an eye roll. It was no use arguing with her father. He and her mother had both poured their lives into Marine World, the small, privately-owned aquarium that specialized in dolphins, holding shows and teaching children as well as looking after injured and rescued dolphins. Now that they were in their sixties, they'd decided it was time for KK to take over. There had been an unspoken understanding for years that KK would take the reins when her parents were ready to move on, but it was only recently that hard plans were put into action. Still, despite the years of learning the ropes and working with the animals, her father still felt obligated to give her advice whenever possible. It would be annoying if it weren't also endearing.

Her dad patted her on the shoulder and then moved to examine the other sling, his normal slight limp more prominent on the rocking boat.

"I'm going to miss these two," he sighed. "But it's time for them to go back."

"We've still got Corey and Carey," KK assured him. The twin dolphins, Majestique and Simon's calves had been born in captivity, unlike their parents. They would stay at the aquarium and take over the majority of the show.

"True, true," her father agreed, bending down as her mother crouched beside him. "Now remember, when you start the show with Corey and Carey, you'll want to..."

The wind pushed his words away from her, and KK turned, effectively tuning him out. She already knew what he was going to say. He'd given her this kind of advice for two years, once they had started laying out the plan for their retirement and her eventual takeover. She stretched and scanned the horizon again as the sun continued its descent. Then her eyes locked on something she hadn't noticed earlier. It was another boat.

There was nothing out of the ordinary about the boat, at least not that she could see from this distance, but the sight still struck her as odd. It was getting dark, and the other boat wasn't making any moves toward shore. In fact, it seemed to be settling down into one location, as if preparing to fish. Her eyes narrowed as an uncomfortable prickling sensation crawled along her back.

"KK, come help," her mother called from the slings. KK pulled her gaze away from the other boat and headed toward the stern.

It took only a few minutes to release Majestique and Simon. They chattered and clicked up at the three humans before diving beneath the water. A minute later, their backs and tails emerged from the water before submerging again.

"I'm going to miss them," Katerina sighed, leaning over the edge of the boat to watch them.

"It was time," Joseph expressed.

They watched in silence, the gentle waves lapping against the side of their boat as they watched the sun continue to sink, the dolphins getting further and further away.

"We should head back before it gets much darker," Joseph suggested, stretching as he looked at his watch.

KK didn't say anything. Her eyes had drifted away from the retreating dolphins and back toward the mysterious boat. Even from this distance, she could tell that it was a large one for fishing, about the size of their own.

"Does anything about that boat strike either of you guys as odd?" she asked, nodding toward the boat.

Her parents glanced toward it. Her father shrugged, but her mother's back stiffened and her chocolate-colored eyes narrowed to slits. Her lips twisted into a suspicious frown.

"It's not exactly a good time of day to be fishing," she remarked, echoing KK's own thoughts.

"It is odd," Joseph agreed, shrugging. "But some people are just weird."

"Joseph," she trilled sharply, in a tone that told everyone not to question or argue with her. "Get me the binoculars."

Her husband obeyed, taking less than a minute to fish them out of a container near the wheel and placing them in Katerina's hand, which was reaching backward in wait. She held them up and sucked in a breath.

"What?" KK asked.

Katerina held out the binoculars and KK snatched them from her mother's hands, slamming them so hard against her eyes that she wondered if she might get bruises later.

"Poachers," her mom hissed.

Chapter Two

"Are you sure?" Joseph asked, doubtfully.

"It's the only thing that makes sense," she retorted. "At this time of night with that big of a boat. And their headlights aren't on. They're trying not to be seen."

KK studied the other boat through the binoculars. Her mother was right and there wasn't a name on the hull, either. All she could make out were men in dark clothing. At least three of them were huddled up near the port bow, as if struggling with something. Her blood began to boil as she white knuckled the binoculars.

"Let's go," KK growled, handing her dad the binoculars before running toward the anchor. "Ow," she gasped, looking down to see that her father's hand had darted out and had tightly clasped around her bicep.

"That's a terrible idea, KK," he warned, concern wavering in his dark eyes. "It's getting dark, we don't know if they're armed, and we don't have any way of stopping them in the first place. It's too dangerous."

"They're grabbing something now," KK insisted. "I saw them trying to grab something. If we don't go after them now we're going to lose them."

"We can report them to the Coast Guard—"

"They'll take an hour to get here and you know it," KK persisted. "By the time they arrive the poachers will be long gone."

Before her father could answer, she extricated her arm from his grip and darted toward the rope dangling off the side. She hauled in the anchor as fast as she could, her adrenaline pumping with a mixture of panic and anger.

"KK—"

"Don't, Joseph," KK's mother cautioned. "She's right and you know it."

There was a grumbled protest from her father that was quickly cut off. KK could only imagine that her mother had given him one of her trademark looks. She heard her father sigh in exasperation.

She pulled up the anchor and all but threw it on the floor as she ran toward the steering wheel. She'd been boating since she'd been old enough to walk across the plank, and it wasn't long before the boat roared back to life and they were charging toward the poachers.

Next to her, KK's mom was fiddling with the radio, talking into it hurriedly before muttering angrily under her breath and trying again.

"No good," Katerina called over the sound of the motor. "I'm not getting anything but static right now."

KK didn't respond, too intent on her quarry to pay much attention to anything else.

A hand rested on her shoulder and KK spun to see her father.

"They're going to be suspicious of a boat flying toward them like this," he told her, with a more determined look in his eyes. "I don't like that you're insisting on doing this. But if we're gonna do it, we should do it right. Otherwise, they'll be gone before we even get close. Slow down," he advised.

She didn't want to listen. KK shook her head, trying to remove her stubborn doubts, for she knew her dad was right. She grimaced and ultimately slowed the boat down until it was pleasantly puttering along.

"Atta girl," Joseph said approvingly.

As they drew near, she realized that her father had been right. Now that they were closer, she could see that the four men were frozen as they watched their boat move closer to them. She could see that two of the men muttered to one another, and one of the men, tall and lanky, moved toward the cockpit.

"Hey there," Joseph called out cheerily, once they were in shouting distance. "Was wondering if you could help.

We're running out of gas and won't be able to make it back to our dock," he lied.

The men were all wearing black ski masks, however, she could see one of them glowering, his teeth barred at her father in a way that made KK's knuckles turn white against the steering wheel.

"Nope," one of the men shouted back. His voice was comically deep and gravelly as if he were intentionally trying to distort it. "Now get lost. You're disturbing the fish."

Something thrashed in the water and made squeaking, clicking sounds that tied a knot in KK's stomach even as it fueled her wrath. Shifting her eyes from the masked man to the sound, the ire doubled in intensity as she saw what was moving in the water.

A dolphin calf.

On the ship she could see two dolphin carcasses, fully grown, unlike the helpless, frightened calf in the net, struggling to break free. Looking at the netting he was trapped in, the knot was cinched too tight. There were nets that were suitable for catching dolphins. This was not one of them. If they didn't do something, that calf would be as good as dead. As if they hadn't already seen what they had done, one of the men was hurriedly trying to cover the calf with a tarp.

"Dad," KK hissed sharply. "The net."

Her father's head instantly snapped to the poacher's net in the water, and his hazel eyes, normally warm and friendly, grew wide with shock at the sight before they narrowed in distaste and an anger that mirrored KK's own.

"I think it might be best for everything involved if you release the calf immediately," her dad commanded. His voice was taut with barely controlled anger as he stared down the men.

On the other boat, the poachers stiffened, looking at one another with alarm as they communicated silently what to do.

"Now!" The man who had spoken earlier, no longer disguising his voice, ordered before KK or her father could react.

The poacher's boat launched into action, peeling away from them, leaving large wakes as they sped off. Without waiting for her parents to say or do anything, KK launched their boat after them. Now she understood why her parents invested so much into a boat. Though she doubted it was to chase down poachers, it was the superior speed and horsepower that made boating alongside the wild dolphins a thrill. The only thrill she'd get now would be to bring those murderous poachers to justice.

"KK, let them go," her father yelled as she forced the boat into pursuit.

"That calf is going to die if we don't cut it free," KK yelled back, keeping her eyes on the struggling baby dolphin. "I'm not letting that happen."

Joseph said something she couldn't quite hear, then her father appeared next to her.

"This is dangerous," he warned, reaching forward toward the steering wheel.

"If you take this wheel from me I'm going to jump and swim after it," she threatened.

"I'm better at maneuvering this boat at speed than you are," he told her, taking the wheel from her and nudging her out of the way.

KK glared at him but didn't argue. Instead, she hurried toward the bow and looked out. Her father was already closing the gap between the two boats. She could see the poor dolphin calf flailing and thrashing in the net in panic. Her heart began to break as she saw how scared it was.

When her father had almost pulled up beside the boat, she couldn't wait any longer. Instead, she grabbed one of the utility knives, placed it between her clenched teeth, and leaped into the water.

Her parents' cries of protest vanished as warm salt water welcomed her into the liquid realm for a brief moment before she resurfaced. Her hand reached out and she barely managed to grab onto the net holding the calf as the rest of the boat continued to move. Her arm screamed in pain as she moved with the boat, holding onto it only by the netting currently biting into her fingers. With the hand not holding on for dear life, she lifted the knife from her mouth and began to cut through the netting, trying to avoid the still-panicking calf.

"Stop her!" Someone on the poacher's boat yelled.

KK glanced up in time to see the butt of a rifle racing toward her. She dodged, letting out a gasp and choking on the salt water that flooded her mouth as she did. Sputtering, she nearly let go of the net, barely managing to hang on. She knew she wouldn't be able to last much longer, not at these speeds. She had to hurry if she had any hope of rescuing the poor thing.

She quickly sliced through the rest of the netting, nearly losing the knife in her haste. Finally, the net fell away from the boat and the calf chittered as it wriggled its way out.

The butt of the rifle slammed toward her again. This time, she did lose the knife as she grabbed the rifle and yanked, pulling the masked poacher into the water.

The man cried out but somehow managed to keep the gun above water even as the other two boats continued to fall away. KK glanced at the boats as her parents began to slowly turn around and head back in their direction. But then agonizing pain slammed into her head as the poacher's rifle finally made contact with KK's head. She flailed backward, everything spinning crazily around her. She heard furious chattering and watched as the dolphin calf began sprinting toward the poacher. There was a gunshot. The calf gave a cry of pain, then knocked the rifle out of the poacher's hands and proceeded to attack the man. KK tried to make a move to help the dolphin, but before she could do anything, she felt her vision go black and her body begin to drop below the surface. Then nothing.

She wasn't sure how much time had passed before her eyes blinked open and she came into a semi-conscious state. Something was dragging her along by her wet suit, and it took KK a minute to realize the dolphin was trying to carry her.

Head still pounding, she wrapped her arm around the dolphin and tried to kick, pushing them toward wherever they were going. When her eyes opened more widely, she realized that they were close to shore. Very close. The fight in the water must have been nearer the island than she realized.

The baby dolphin got her as near the beach as possible. KK staggered upward when she felt sand beneath her feet. Then she turned to look at the calf and her heart lurched.

There was a bullet wound on the edge of his fin, a bleeding notch. The dolphin looked up at her and chattered at her. He looked pleased with himself, even if he was injured.

"You saved me," she croaked, disbelief etching every syllable. She'd worked with dolphins her entire life, but something like that...she'd never seen anything like that. Not even with Majestique or Simon.

But anything else she wanted to say to the dolphin was wiped away from her brain when she saw movement out of the corner of her eye.

Sucking in a breath, she turned just in time to see a man in dark clothing climbing out of the water, panting heavily. Even from here, she could hear him swearing loudly. The man grabbed the top of his mask and yanked it off in a fury.

Then, before KK could do or say anything, he looked in her direction. KK's stomach clenched in dread as their eyes met. The man snarled and took a step toward her. Then voices come from further down the beach.

"Keiko??"

It was her mother. Her parents must have docked nearby. The poacher glowered at her one last time, before running away.

KK stumbled toward the shore, head still throbbing and everything spinning. Her arm and fingers hurt, and she knew the goose egg on her head was only going to grow bigger.

Her mother was still calling her name by the time KK had finally pulled herself out of the tide and onto wet sand. The sky was dark, but she was fairly certain that the stars spinning around her head weren't the normal kind.

She was just about to call out to her mother when everything faded and she fell. She blacked out just before she hit the sand.

Three

Chapter Three

Her eyes were heavy and crusty, and her entire body was comfortably warm and dry. She considered falling back asleep, but then voices filtered through the blackness.

"She'll be up soon," a familiar female voice said. "There's no way she'll miss the start of construction."

"I don't think she has a lot of choice in it, Nikki," remarked another familiar voice, this one male. "I don't think injuries particularly care if you have something coming up."

"Wish they did," KK muttered, peeling her eyes open. "I'd tell this migraine that I had a date and ask it to reschedule."

She managed to force the weighted blanket from her eyelids and found four faces staring back at her, all with identical expressions of ecstatic relief.

She was in a hospital room. Sterile white walls surrounded her with bland photos and a window. A curtain was drawn to her right, which meant someone was probably there. To her left was a door opening onto a tiled hallway. She could feel tight bandages wrapped around her head and she winced as she poked at it.

"I don't think you're supposed to poke at it," Tony reckoned. KK made a face and he grinned.

"One of these days you're going to stop acting like a big brother," she grumbled.

"Maybe on a day when you don't wind up in the hospital," Tony retorted, still grinning. "But I'm glad you're okay."

He reached out and squeezed her hand, and KK smiled. She'd known Tony since they were kids, and even though he was now her employee, he still remained one of her closest friends. It was no wonder he was one of the first ones here.

"Honestly, though, I kind of want to hit you in the head again after your parents told me how you wound up in the hospital. Jumping off a moving boat to go after poachers?" He shook his head exasperatedly.

"I was jumping off a moving boat to rescue a calf," KK corrected, pushing herself into a seated position as she looked at the others huddled around her. Nikki was seated next to Tony, her red hair falling down one shoulder. Normally, she wasn't the easiest to read, but the relief in her eyes was obvious. On the other side of the bed were two other women: Reese and Pamela. Reese, a beautiful, middle-aged woman was beaming with relief down at KK. Pamela was scowling, but it was the scowl Pamela always used when she was happy.

Nikki shook her head, her red hair swishing with the movement. "You've always been one to jump first and ask questions later when it comes to animals in trouble," she teased.

"So what happened exactly?" Tony asked. The three women nodded, all of them leaning forward eagerly to listen.

KK opened her mouth to tell them the story. Then paused. Blinked. Closed her mouth. Her brow furrowed, then she winced in pain as the bruise stretched with the motion. "I... don't remember," she finally moaned. "I remember releasing Majestique and Simon and then going after the other boat. I remember seeing that there was a calf trapped in a net and..." She trailed off, shaking her head and instantly regretting it when the room began to spin. "After that, I don't remember anything."

"That's so weird," Nikki commented, her eyes wide. Her eyes lit up. "Oh my god, I should text Justin about this!"

Pamela scoffed, not bothering to hide her annoyance while KK and Tony exchanged amused glances. Ever since Nikki had gotten married a couple of months earlier, she talked about her new husband Justin whenever she got the chance, much to the amusement of the other employees at the aquarium and to the annoyance of Pamela. Pamela, despite being quite possibly the best wedding planner on the island, had strong opinions on the matter of marriage ever since her divorce a few years earlier. Despite that, she still was borderline obsessive when it came to other people's weddings. She'd even planned Nikki's. You would think that Pamela would be flattered by the fact that Nikki raved about how perfect the wedding was on a regular basis. To be honest, she probably was, Pamela just liked grumbling too much to admit it.

"How long have I been out?" KK asked.

"Your parents found you on the beach last night," Reese told her. "It's a little before nine in the morning right now."

"Nine in the..." She trailed off, then glanced at Nikki and Tony. "Who's at the aquarium? Mom and Dad?"

"They're outside," Reese pointed behind her. "We had to fight them to get in here for a couple of hours."

"Someone needs to look after the animals if they haven't been fed yet." KK moved as if to get up, and Tony and Reese both pushed her gently back to the bed.

"Of course you're more worried about the aquarium than you are the fact that you nearly died last night," Tony said, shaking his head. His hand went to her arm and he squeezed gently. "Relax. Deb and Tim are looking after things."

That didn't relax her at all, but before she could ask any more questions, Reese was speaking again.

"Your parents told us all about it," she shared. "I'm pretty sure they're furious with you for jumping into the water from a moving boat. Apparently they came across you after you had passed out and brought you here. Though I wouldn't have found out if Nikki hadn't told me." Reese shot KK a glare, as if it were her fault for not telling Reese she had been concussed and knocked out the entire night, despite the fact that she'd been, well, knocked out.

Reese was still talking. "Anyway, I got here as fast as I could, and when I got here the nurse said I couldn't come in, that there were already too many people in the room—"

"Let her rest," Pamela ordered, her German accent even more prominent than normal. She bent down and grabbed something that had been sitting beneath her chair, a small rectangular container. "Here, I brought you a treat."

She opened the box to reveal mouthwatering malasadas, a Hawaiian donut. KK's stomach rumbled at the sight and the smell of freshly baked dough and sugar made her stomach growl.

"Uncle Senior?" she asked, plucking one from the box and stuffing it in her mouth. She moaned at the taste of the haupia filling. It was quite possibly the best tasting thing she'd had in a week, or at least since she'd last had Uncle Senior's malasadas.

"Naturally," Pamela sniffed. "I only buy from the best."

"I think you're just obsessed with them," Nikki chuckled. "You basically forced me to have them as a dessert option at my wedding."

"Of course I did." Pamela looked almost confused. "Your wedding needed to be perfect, didn't it?"

Again, KK exchanged an amused glance with Tony, both of them pursing their lips to stop themselves from giggling. At this point, KK was surprised Pamela hadn't tried to marry Uncle Senior just so she could have unlimited access to her favorite treat.

As Pamela plucked out one of the malasadas for herself, a middle-aged man in scrubs and a doctor's coat came in.

"Hi there," he greeted, holding out his hand to KK. "Glad to see you're awake. I'm Dr. Kanoa."

"Keiko Kawai," she replied back with a small smile, shaking his hand. "KK."

"So I've heard." He glanced around at the group of people huddled around her bed. "I do need to take care of my patient, and I'm fairly certain her parents are foaming at the mouth in the waiting room to see her, so I'm sorry but I'm going to have to ask you to step out."

"Of course." Tony stood, as did the three women. He glanced at KK. "I'll see you soon, all right?"

"We all will," Nikki chimed in. "Just don't go after any more poachers until after you're out of the hospital."

KK snorted. "Deal."

Dr. Kanoa looked her over quickly and expertly, before standing again, once everyone had shuffled out of the room.

"Well you have a major contusion on the side of your head, and while I'm worried about the loss of consciousness, the CT shows no signs of concussion. You should be good to go home tomorrow," the doctor confirmed. "We'll keep you here for the day and release you first thing tomorrow."

"Fantastic," KK sighed, laying back so her head was resting on the pillow. "I hate being cooped up like this."

"You're not the first person to say that to me," Kanoa chuckled. "I'll have the nurse come in and check on you later. In the meantime, I can tell your parents to come in, if you want to see them."

KK nodded, and not two minutes after the doctor had vanished, both her parents hurried into the room. Katerina's wavy brown hair was frizzy and unkempt, and her father had large bags under his eyes. KK felt a stab of guilt for making them worry so much.

"Oh thank goodness you're okay," Katerina gushed, hugging her daughter. "Don't you ever do something that stupid again."

"I'll do my best, Mom," KK promised, breathing in the lilac smell of her mother's perfume. "In my defense, I wasn't exactly thinking things through."

"I know," her mother said, her lips pursing even as her eyes sparkled with relief. She leaned forward and whispered, almost conspiratorially, "You get that from your father."

"I don't know what you're talking about," Joseph claimed, hugging KK. "I'm the perfect soul of caution. And I have definitely never jumped off a moving boat."

"What about that time in our twenties off the coast of Kauai?" Katerina asked, folding her arms as she eyed her husband.

"Okay, so I might have done it once or twice. But I was never chasing after armed poachers while doing it."

"Sorry," KK muttered.

"We're just glad you're alright," Katerina grinned. "Um, that reminds me. A detective is in the waiting room as well. We filed a report and he wants to talk to you, if you're feeling up for it."

"Absolutely." KK nodded with renewed energy. "Anything to bring those poachers to justice."

The man who walked in behind her father looked young to be a detective. Maybe it was the round face or the unassuming posture, but he didn't exactly scream 'law enforcement.' Then his brown eyes met hers, and the intensity in his gaze made her completely disregard that impression.

"Hey there," he said, smiling. "I'm Detective Max Kremer. You must be Keiko."

"KK," she insisted. "But yeah, that's me."

"Your parents told me a bit about what happened," he started, gesturing over to where Katerina and Joseph were standing. "However I was hoping you could tell me what you remember."

KK gave an amused snort. "I can't tell you much," she sighed. "I don't remember a lot of it." With that, she told him what she could, and as she did, she found that more of her memories came back. Not all of them. She couldn't remember what the poacher looked like or anything like that, but enough to at least remember how she wound up on the beach instead of drowning in the ocean.

"I think the little dolphin..." she trailed off, then her eyes shot open, and she gasped. "The dolphin calf! He was hurt. We need to find him."

"It's okay sweetie," her mother soothed. "We found him. When we found you on the beach he was in the ocean nearby. He refused to go anywhere until he knew you were safe. Your father managed to get him and take him to the aquarium where our vet is looking after him now."

"He's going to be alright?" KK asked anxiously. Her parents looked at one another but said nothing.

"Can you guys think of any reason people would want to poach dolphins?" Detective Kremer asked, momentarily distracting KK. She gave her parents a long, speculative look before answering Kremer's question.

"Mostly for bait or food," KK grimaced. "It's pretty disgusting."

"Bait?"

"Sharks," KK clarified. "Poach something illegal so you can do more illegal fishing." She shifted in her bed, wincing slightly as she did, to get a better look at her parents. "The calf is going to be alright, isn't he?"

She hated the look that flashed between her parents at the question. It didn't take a genius to know what they were thinking. The idea that the little calf might not make it was enough to chill any of the good humor her friends had given her.

"We don't know, sweetie," Katerina said gently. "We hope so. But right now he's so depressed it's hard to tell. He's barely swimming and he won't eat on top of the injury. We don't know if he'll make it."

KK's eyes narrowed and she gritted her teeth.

"He will," she avowed. "I'm going to make sure of it."

Chapter Four

When KK walked into the dolphin area of the aquarium, it was just in time to see a beautiful young dolphin leaping out of the water over and over again, the morning sun glistening on her back.

"Come on, Carey, one more," a deep voice commanded. KK looked over to see an attractive black man standing on the rocks, holding a fish in one hand as he watched the dolphin. He made a gesture with his hand. "I know you can do it."

Carey jumped again, this time diving deep and not reemerging until she was right in front of Tim. He grinned broadly.

"Good girl," he praised. "Now, I've got one more fish for you if you stay right where you are."

Carey trilled but waited patiently. KK watched as Tim pulled a phone from his pocket, crouched and held it up so that both he and the dolphin would be in view. He must have taken a dozen photos before standing again.

"Oh, that's a good one," he praised, tossing the fish toward the dolphin without really looking. "That'll get a thousand likes in the first ten minutes easy."

"What did I tell you about using the dolphins in photos?" KK called playfully from where she stood.

Tim's head shot up, and he flashed KK a dazzling grin that showed not a single hint of remorse.

"Would you believe me if I said it would be good for business?" he asked, walking across the rocks to where a set of metal steps descended to the concrete floor of the open-air arena. "I can tag Marine World in every one of my posts.

"That would be a great excuse," KK said, folding her arms. "If we had an Instagram or a TikTok."

"Which you should!" he exclaimed. "Do you realize how much more business you'd get? The place is popular already but if you put up a couple of live feeds of some of the animals or got a strong social media base it would probably double. And now that you're in charge, you don't have to argue with your parents about it anymore." His eyes lit up. "I could totally manage it if you want. No pay increase or anything."

"Uh-huh. In exchange for what?"

"Just letting me take photos with the animals and use the aquarium in my own posts." His voice raised an octave and he spoke rather quickly, as if trying to be more dismissive of the idea. She snorted.

"It's something that's crossed my mind," she admitted. "And trust me. If I trust anyone to handle the social media side, it'll be you. Just as long as you keep training the animals. You're too good at that for me to let you stop."

Tim's grin widened, his dark eyes sparkling. "Trust me, I'll convince you sooner or later." He glanced down at his phone and beamed. "See? Three hundred likes in about five minutes."

KK peered over at his phone, which showed the handsome, dark-skinned man posing with Carey.

"That is pretty impressive," she admitted. "Sometimes I don't get why you work here with the number of followers you have."

"Two reasons." He held up two fingers. "One, I like it here and get bored easily."

"And the second?"

"Do you realize how many amazing photos I get of this place? My follower count practically doubled when I started working here."

Timothy Shemlock, who goes by Tim, had come from California about a year ago. He'd worked at SeaWorld on the mainland but moved to Oahu after some accusations of climbing the ranks through unsavory methods. KK had never fully gotten an explanation as to what those were, but based on how well he worked with the animals, she didn't particularly care as long as he toed the line here. Which, with the exception of taking too many selfie breaks, he had. He might be an obnoxious know-it-all on certain subjects, but he tended to back it up with legitimate knowledge.

"By the way," he continued, glancing over at her. "I'm thrilled you're back, don't get me wrong. But shouldn't you be resting more? Tony told me what happened."

KK glared at him. "Please don't go down that road," she pleaded, slumping her shoulders.

"Just saying, if you've been concussed, you're supposed to take it easy."

"You should know that's never going to happen," another voice chimed in from behind KK. She turned to see Deborah, the children's coordinator, walking toward them. "She's never going to take a break unless someone ties her down."

"That's because there's too much to do," KK pointed out. "We have the first show with the twins without their parents in a few days. We need to make sure they're ready."

"They will be," Deborah assured her. "We've been training them well. But..." she hesitated, glancing over at Tim.

"But what?"

"It might not be the best idea to have the show until we've figured out what to do with the calf," Deborah suggested. "He's kind of taking up a lot of our time at the moment."

KK's stomach lurched. This plus the new renovations going on plus the upcoming show displaying the twin dolphins, Carey and Corey for the first time without their parents was the last thing she needed. She already felt so overwhelmed. And that's not including the concussion, she thought miserably.

"How is he doing?" she asked.

"Not good," Tony admitted. "He's pretty listless, and with that bullet wound..." he trailed off.

"People are thinking it might be best to put him down," KK sighed. After everything she had gone through to save the little guy, she didn't know if she would be able to handle watching the calf die.

"Rosie is here," Deborah announced. "She'd know better than either of us."

Rosie Stevens, the woman the aquarium always called when there might be a problem with one of their animals. It was no surprise her parents had gotten in touch with her. KK nodded. "Right," she acknowledged, moving past Tim to get to the staff-only area. "Let me put on my wetsuit."

They had a small isolation tank that they used for new animals to make sure they weren't sick and to help them get acclimated to their new environment. That would be where the calf would be. Sure enough, when KK strolled through the halls and out to where the special tank was,

Rosie, a young, petite woman with dirty blond hair and a vivacious personality, was there with a clipboard. She turned.

"Hey there, KK," she greeted. She jerked her head toward the tank. "Heard you two saved one another."

"Pretty much."

She walked over to stand next to Rosie, looking into the tank at the baby dolphin. He looked so small in the tank, and he was barely swimming. His wounded fin looked better, and he was still able to move it, but the listless way he moved in the water was heartbreaking. If he were human, it would be a textbook example of depression. KK sighed.

"Poor guy," Rosie said sympathetically.

"Yeah," sighed KK, watching him. "I'm going to hop in the tank and see what happens."

Rosie's eyes flashed with surprise and alarm. "Are you sure that's the best idea?" she asked. "I mean, we don't know how he'll react."

"He saved my life in the water," KK told her. "I don't remember much, but I remember that at least. "I think I'll be fine."

Rosie opened her mouth as if to protest again, but closed it when she caught sight of KK's expression. She fell silent.

KK walked around and climbed to the edge of the tank, where a metal overhang allowed her to sit. Her feet and calves dangled in the water, making gentle ripples. The water was pleasantly warm, adjusted to what would be most comfortable to the little dolphin who was now watching KK with unnerving intensity. A jolt rippled through her as intelligent, black eyes regarded her. The calf stopped. And something about the way he was looking at her reminded her of someone cocking their head.

After a moment to make sure the baby dolphin wasn't going to attack her while on the edge of the tank, she slid in. The moment she did, the dolphin swam immediately up to her. KK heard Rosie gasp from outside the tank as if worried that the dolphin was preparing to attack. But inside the water, KK was entranced.

The calf stopped right in front of her for a brief moment, then bridged the final gap, and nuzzled against her shoulder. Gentle clicks came from his mouth as KK's mouth dropped open.

"Hey there," she cooed. And, without realizing she was doing it, she wrapped her arms around the dolphin, stroking him gently.

The calf's eyes brightened and he moved to nudge her hand, almost like a cat demanding pets. His eyes brightened, the clicking and chittering growing more enthusiastic. It was as if he was coming back to life.

He nuzzled against her one more time before swimming off, diving below the surface. KK stood where she was, and a moment later, the calf shot into the air as gracefully as Majestique or Simon. He did it again and again, before coming back to KK. This time, he stopped a ways back. He looked at her again, then, before she could react, turned, and slapped his tail, sending a wave of water splashing across KK's face. She laughed in shock, and she could swear the dolphin laughed with her.

"He wants to play," KK smiled, unable to hide her delight. Seeing the calf happy and lively meant more to her than she could ever describe. A bizarre jolt of familiarity, as if she'd known this dolphin for years and not a handful of minutes, shot through her with such intensity it was nearly overwhelming.

"Throw me a ball," KK shouted to Rosie, who watched from the other side of the tank with undisguised amazement. "There are some in that crate over there."

A moment later, a white ball the size of a melon landed in the water. Before KK could even grab it, the calf lunged for it, grabbing it in his mouth and swimming away in delight. He glanced over at KK, and she realized he wanted her to chase after her.

Grinning like a maniac, her throbbing head completely forgotten, she swam toward him, only for him to dart away, chittering merrily even as he held the ball in his mouth.

"Come on, let me throw it," KK urged the little guy.

As if he understood her, the calf dropped the ball, nudging it toward her enthusiastically. KK grabbed it and threw it halfway across the tank and he dove after it, grabbing it just before KK reached it. This time, he dropped it almost instantly, waiting for her to toss it again.

It was as if he had an entire change in his whole personality. The wound on his fin didn't seem to bother him at all as they swam around the tank and played. After maybe ten minutes, during which Rosie watched on, her mouth open, KK paused. And she knew that she would never let anyone put this calf down ever. She adored all animals, especially the ones in the aquarium that she had looked after nearly her whole life, but she had never felt such a connection with any of them as she felt with this calf.

"You should get some rest, buddy," KK said as the dolphin swam up to her, nuzzling her once more. "I've got some other work to do. Like filling out all the paperwork to make sure you can stay here."

As if he understood her, the dolphin clicked excitedly.

"You're keeping him?" Rosie asked.

KK nodded, petting the dolphin with both hands. "Gotta come up with a name for you, though, buddy," she muttered to him. As she thought, her gaze went to the healing wound on his fin, and righteous anger flooded through her at the sight. She glowered at it, thinking back to what had happened, how this calf had saved her life by not only taking her to shore but defending her from the man in the water. And she knew what she was going to call him.

"His name is Jasper," she confirmed. "It means treasure. Because he treasured my life enough to risk his." Her teeth clenched as she continued to lovingly stroke the calf. "And we have some poachers to kill."

Chapter Five

Corey and Carey jumped into the air in perfect harmony, before diving so elegantly that they barely made a splash. An Olympic diver couldn't have done better.

"Great job!" KK praised, tossing both of them a fish from where she stood on the rocks. She made a spinning motion with her hands, and the twins submerged again. This time, she watched as they looped and swam in the water like a complicated dance. She glanced over at Tim, who was at ground level watching the dolphins through the glass panels in the tank.

"How do they look?" she asked.

"A little out of sync," Tim admitted, studying the dolphin's movements. "Corey is cutting corners and going too fast."

KK made a face but nodded. "Sounds like him," she murmured, running her fingers through damp hair. Their first show was scheduled for next week, and it felt like there was so much to do. It kept feeling as though more things were getting piled up instead of getting taken care of.

"Hey, KK?"

Nikki had appeared at the far end of the training arena and was walking toward her.

"What's up?"

"There's a detective here for you," Nikki reported. "He said it was about what happened last month. I told him to wait in your office."

"All right, thanks." She glanced over at Tim. "You got it from here?" she asked.

Tim nodded, already pulling his phone back out of his pocket to check for notifications.

Marine World was relatively small. There was a backstage area, where the isolation tank is, as well as a larger tank where the dolphins sometimes stay. It also had the training arena, an indoor show arena, and the outdoors arena. Almost all the tanks were connected by tubes that the dolphins could swim through to get from one to the other, and those tubes could be blocked off during showtime or if they wanted to separate the dolphins for any reason.

She walked by the tank where Jasper was swimming lazily. He had been moved out of the isolation tank, but she was still keeping him away from Corey and Carey for the time being. He watched her as she strolled past, swimming up against the glass as she walked as if he were escorting her.

"Good to see you, too," she said. "I'll come by later with some fish."

Jasper rose to the surface and air exploded from his blowhole in a way that clearly said you better. KK chuckled and continued walking toward her office at the far end of the backstage area.

When she opened the door, Detective Kremer, the officer from the hospital, was standing up, reading one of the newspaper clippings that KK's parents had clipped and framed when this had been their office. The walls were covered in clippings praising the aquarium as well as photos of the various dolphins they had taken in and rescued over the years, as well as the ones they had nursed back to health before releasing. The office itself was cozy and a little cluttered, with a large desk at the far end and a small window looking out at the outdoor arena. The filing cabinet in the corner was in desperate need of clearing out, and she really needed to neaten up her desk. She closed the door and the detective turned toward her.

"How can I help you, Detective Kremer?" she asked. "Is there an update on the investigation?"

Ever since she had been released from the hospital, she had been waiting with bated breath for any word on the poachers. Her heart pounded excitedly as she waited for him to tell her it was all over, that they'd caught the men.

He gave a long sigh. "Unfortunately, no. There hasn't been anything. There haven't been any other reports of poachers in this area or anything that might point us to who attacked you."

Her heart sank and her shoulders slumped. Her lips pursed in an almost uncanny resemblance to her mother.

"Nothing?" she demanded. He shook his head.

"I wish I could tell you otherwise," he shrugged. "I really do. But it isn't that simple."

"He hit me over the head with the butt of a gun," KK exclaimed. "I nearly drowned."

"I know. And I want to make sure we catch the guy. I came here to ask if you can remember anything at all."

KK let out a long exhalation and squeezed her eyes shut to try and remember. Nothing new resurfaced, it was all the same fog. She shook her head in frustration.

"Nothing," she said bitterly. "Absolutely nothing.

Kremer looked disappointed, though not necessarily surprised. He nodded. "In that case, I need to get going," he replied. "Let me know if you remember anything later."

"Do you think they just don't care?" Deborah asked when KK finished relating the conversation she'd had with the detective. The calf was elated, jumping over and over again each time she threw him a fish. "Because it's really starting to feel like they don't care."

Detective Kremer had left a little while ago, but the bitterness over the lack of news had stuck with KK and it was hard not to disagree with her employee's sentiment. She sighed as she tossed another fish high in the air.

"I hope not," she breathed.

"You're more optimistic than I am, then," Deborah grumbled. Unlike KK, she was dressed in what they might call their 'teacher uniform,' khaki shorts and a blue polo with the Marine World logo—a dolphin leaping over the words—stitched over the left breast. There was a class coming in soon. Though Deborah wasn't a fan of helping with the shows and used every excuse imaginable to get out of them, she was incredible with children, her normally standoffish personality evaporating as she taught kids about dolphins.

"I'm more optimistic than you in a lot of departments," KK smiled sweetly.

Nikki, who had been walking toward Carey and Corey's tanks, stopped when she overheard the conversation.

"Seriously? They didn't come up with anything?" Nikki demanded.. Her eyes blazed with anger and protectiveness. "Those jerks."

Her anger wasn't surprising in the slightest. Ever since Nikki had arrived on the island after moving from the mainland, there had been an instant connection between the two of them, and it had only solidified since into best friends.

"There isn't a whole lot I can do to change it," KK trailed off as Nikki hopped up to stand next to her on the overhang.

"Well it still sucks," she grumbled. "How's the new kid doing?"

"He's doing well," KK smiled. "Though he still seems a bit skittish."

"He doesn't look it now," Nikki noticed, jerking her head over to where Jasper was swimming happily, twisting and turning in the water gracefully like he was dancing with himself. "He looks like he's doing great."

"He's fine when he's with me," KK amended. "But as soon as you bring someone else into it, he gets grumpy."

"Nah, I'm sure it's fine." To emphasize her point, Nikki walked over to the edge of the overhang and leaned forward. "Isn't it, Jasper?"

Jasper paused his acrobatics and eyed Nikki distrustfully. He gave a series of warning clicks, his eyes never leaving Nikki.

"I don't think he wants you near him at the moment," KK warned.

"He's probably just tired," Nikki proposed. "Or it's the injury in his fin acting up."

The injury was almost fully healed at this point, though the notch in the fin would always be there. Regardless, KK doubted that the injury was affecting his mood at the moment.

"He's just getting used to people," KK cautioned with a hint of worry in her voice. Jasper had gotten better, at least with her, but the fact was he still had a long way to go, and it was a little concerning seeing how long a road they had ahead of them.

"Anyway, I've got to get over to Corey and Carey," Nikki said, finally backing off. "We'll get this guy in the show in no time. Reese is here, by the way. She wanted to see how the renovations were going."

KK slapped her forehead. "I totally forgot she was coming today," she grimaced. "Thanks, Nikki. I'll see you later."

Reese was sitting on one of the concrete stands in the outdoor arena staring down at her phone, texting rapidly as KK approached. Her forehead was creased in annoyance.

"Everything all right?" KK asked.

"Oh, it's fine," Reese gave a smile that didn't hide her annoyance all that well. "Jacob wants his girlfriend to come over this weekend even after I told him we already had plans."

"Jacob has a girlfriend?" Reese barely spoke of her son, so KK always took any opportunity she could to get information on him.

"He says girlfriend," Reese rolled her eyes. "You know how fifteen-year-olds are. Now, I want to see what you're doing with all that land I got for you."

And that was the end of their conversation about Jacob. Reese may be one of KK's best friends, but the older woman kept her private life as private as it was possible to get, with a few exceptions.

"It's coming along," KK replied, gesturing for Reese to follow her as they walked around the complex toward the back area. "The general contractor says things are ahead of schedule, though they've needed to make adjustments to some of my ideas in order for it to work."

"Sounds about right."

A few minutes later, the two of them arrived at a construction site. Steel columns had been erected and stuck into the cement foundation. Eventually, this whole area would be what KK liked to imagine as 'The Sanctuary,' an employee's only area to decompress and get away from the hecticness of the rest of Marine World. She had envisioned stone walkways and a koi pond with plenty of greenery. Right now, it was just a slab of concrete, but when it was done, it would be absolutely stunning.

"Not bad," Reese commented, nodding.

"It's pretty bland to look at right now," KK sighed. "But it's going to look amazing once it's finished."

"Oh I have no doubt," Reese chuckled, flashing KK a grin. "I know you well enough to know you don't do things by halves. This is going to be great when it's all said and done."

"Well, I have you to thank for that even being a possibility at all."

A couple of years ago, once KK's parents had begun their slow start to retirement, KK had brought up the idea of the Sanctuary, something she had been imagining for years. She had started looking for real estate people in the area so that she could buy the land around Marine World to build it, and had come across Reese. Not only had Reese been able to get them an amazing deal on a large piece of oceanfront property adjacent to the aquarium, but she had also become fast friends with KK. It didn't take long before they were spending time together outside of business meetings, and when KK had introduced Reese to Nikki and Pamela, friendships had fallen into place.

The two of them walked around the area for a bit, KK pointing out where things were going to be and debating whether or not buying other nearby land would be a good idea for expanding Marine World in the future. After an hour or so of this, the two of them headed toward the tanks. Reese wanted to meet Jasper.

When they got there, KK was surprised to see Tim on the side of the tank in a wetsuit, crouching down as he watched Jasper swim. On the concrete floor, Tony was leaning against a mop handle, watching the scene. He startled when KK approached.

"Miss anything?" she asked.

"Nothing yet," Tony stipulated, glancing back at the tank. "Not a whole lot going on at the moment."

"Is that why you're staring at Jasper instead of cleaning the training tank like I asked?" KK asked, folding her arms and raising an eyebrow as she looked at the very dry mop in his hands and the lack of any kind of sudsy water bucket.

Tony's cheeks flushed pink. "I was going to get to it," he muttered. Then he poked her with the edge of the mop like a little brother might. "Why does it have to be me?"

"Because you clean them better than anyone," KK mused, batting her eyelashes in mock flattery. "And you complain the least."

He blinked in surprise. "What are you talking about? I complain all the time."

"I said you complained the least, not that you didn't complain." She nudged him.

Tony grumbled and looked like he was about to say something, but KK turned her attention back to the water, where Jasper was slowly moving closer to the edge of the tank as if wanting to get closer to KK.

"He's so handsome," Reese sighed as she watched him. "And he's doing better?"

"He's doing...okay," KK responded.

"I was about to hop in and see if he would play any," Tim said from up top. "But I'm thinking I should hold off. He doesn't seem like he's in the mood for playing."

Jasper, whose attention had been focused mostly on KK this time, swiveled his attention toward Reese. His dark eyes studied her as he floated in the water.

"Hey there, little guy—" Reese began.

Jasper darted toward the top of the water with surprising speed, leaping up into the air. Then, before any of them could do anything, Jasper's tail slapped against the water, sending a wave over the edge of the tank and straight onto Reese.

Reese gasped as the tepid water sunk into her clothing. Tony and Tim looked alarmed as Reese stood there, her fine clothes and faux leather purse dripping with water. From the tank, Jasper let out a string of merry, chipper, chittering sounds.

After a long moment, KK began to laugh. She couldn't help herself.

"I guess he's in a playful mood after all," Reese said, flatly, blinking the water off her lashes.

It was the type of breakthrough she'd been hoping for with Jasper for a while. Up until now, the only playfulness she had seen was with her. The fact that he wanted to play with others as well was more than she could have hoped for.

Though she did wish that Reese hadn't had to sacrifice her clothes for the occasion.

Tony and Tim joined in the laughter, the sound filling the echoing room. After a moment, Reese reluctantly laughed, too.

Chapter Six

"I can't work the show," Deborah pleaded, then gave a loud, fake cough. "I, uh, have a hoarse throat."

KK raised an eyebrow, smiling slightly as she crossed her arms. "You seemed perfectly fine earlier today."

"I must have caught something from my pet," she continued.

"Annabelle?" KK asked.

"Yeah."

"Your hamster?"

Deborah, to her credit, didn't even blink. "Yes."

KK sighed. "Deborah, you know that's not—"

"You can say whatever you like," Deborah chimed in, interrupting. "Just know that if you have me presenting I'm going to talk with a hoarse voice the entire time."

KK tried to stare the woman down, but Deborah's pale features and dark eyes didn't waver as they looked levelly at her boss.

"Alright, alright," KK sighed. "One of these days I'm going to convince you to get up there and actually help with the show. For now, can you at least stay off to the side and keep an eye on Jasper? I want him to watch from the side tank."

"Are people going to come and ask me questions?" Deborah asked.

"If they do, you can talk to them in a hoarse voice to your heart's content," KK surmised. She glanced at the clock on her computer. "I've got to go get ready."

An hour later, the outdoor arena was filled with people sitting on the concrete seats, the air filled with the sound of excited conversation.

KK's mother had preferred to stand off to the side with a hand mic. Now that KK was leading the show, she elected for a waterproof headset, since she also worked with the dolphins.

She strolled up to Tony, who was near the tank.

"Everything good?" she asked.

"Yeah, I think so." He jerked his head over to the side tank, where Jasper was swimming idly. He saw KK looking and he instantly moved toward the glass nearest her, clicking and chattering as if begging to play with her. "He wasn't happy with Deborah leading him into that tank. I don't think he likes taking orders all that much."

"He'll get used to it," she said.

"If anyone can get him acclimated, it's you," he smiled. "I still remember you somehow training your goldfish to do flips in the water."

KK giggled. "I'd forgotten about that," she said. "Though I think that might have been pure luck."

"Nah, where's the fun in thinking that?" He nudged her shoulder. It was clearly trying to be playful, but something about his hesitancy made it more awkward than it should have been. "You are clearly the Dr. Dolittle of the ocean."

KK snorted. "I wish." She glanced at her watch. "Gotta go."

"Good luck!" Tony called after her as she hopped up the steps. She waved back to him in thanks and acknowledgment.

"Hi everyone, and welcome to Marine World!" KK began as the crowd fell silent. "It's great to have you guys here, and I know two of the Marine World's residents who are very excited to see you as well."

On silent cue, Carey and Corey arced through the air from opposite sides of the tank, soaring high overhead and crossing midair. The audience cheered excitedly, clapping as the two dolphins landed.

KK smiled, scanning the audience. It was mostly families with young children. A couple of groups of high schoolers and couples on dates were scattered throughout as well. Some were locals, but enough of them had those telltale tourist signs – bright shirts, hats, looking just a bit out of place with the darker-skinned native Hawai'ians like KK and Tony – that gave them away.

As she looked around the audience watching Carey and Corey playing, her gaze locked on one face in particular. The man had light brown hair, the stubble along his face a similar color. He had intense eyes, and they seemed to be focused right on KK. Something about him caused her to seize up, and an unpleasant prickling sensation, like insects beneath her skin, crawled up her spine. Even with him sitting down, there was something about his posture that was familiar, and she didn't like the way he was staring her down.

She shook her head and pushed him to the back of her mind. She didn't have time to fixate on him today, not during the show.

"We've got a great show for you today, and we hope that, by the time you leave, you'll have learned a bit about our mission here and some cool facts about dolphins that you didn't know."

She flung two fish in the air and the twins scooted backward, their bodies in the air as they propelled themselves gracefully with their fins. Through the rest of the show, they performed, KK sneaking in interesting facts in between the twins' remarkable feats of acrobatics. They really were incredible at this. Off to one side, Jasper floated at the edge of his tank, watching with rapt fascination, as if he wanted to join in on the fun. *One day, buddy*, KK thought, smiling warmly.

Even as she led the show, running Carey and Corey through their familiar routine that still always managed to dazzle KK, she could still feel a gaze boring into her, as if trying to kill her with a glare. She knew exactly where it was coming from, too, and she forced herself not to look at the stranger.

It wasn't until nearly the end of the show when it hit her, shocking her so much that she faltered halfway through a speech about Marine World's mission to help protect the ocean and preserve all marine life as well as rehabilitating dolphins. A memory slammed into her like a punch to the stomach: a man climbing out of the water as he yanked off a mask, shooting her a death glare before he ran from the beach.

The poacher!

Her head swiveled toward where the poacher had been sitting in the stands, momentarily forgetting the fact that she was surrounded by people. Unfortunately, the man was gone, and a quick scan showed that he was nowhere to be seen in the crowd.

She managed to finish the show, soothing herself by telling herself that he had just left. And even if he hadn't, there was no way that he could do anything with all these people around. That didn't stop her from hurrying offstage the moment she was able.

"The poacher was here," she hissed to Tony when she got down from the tank.

Tony's eyes widened. "Are you sure?" he asked. "I thought you couldn't remember what he looked like."

She hesitated. "Okay, I think I saw the poacher," she amended. "And the fact that he left halfway through the show I feel like helps to prove my point."

"I'll keep an eye out for anything suspicious," he promised. "And I'll radio the others. In the meantime, you should probably get out of that wetsuit." He blushed. "As nice as it looks on you, it's not good to stay in wet clothes for too long."

She glared. "Little brothering me again, eh?"

He shrugged, giving a grin as he nudged her playfully. "I just want to make sure you don't get sick," he retorted. "I don't think the aquarium could function without you."

Grinning and rolling her eyes, she hurried back to the backstage area. As annoying as he could be sometimes, he was right.

Once she was back in her normal work clothes, she went back to her office and found a note taped to her door. Someone must need her somewhere. But who? They all carried radios so it wasn't as though they weren't able to get into contact with her easily.

She tugged the sheet of paper off the opaque window and read it. It was short, and it made her earlier anxiety feel like a blip on the radar.

Don't think I don't know who you are. We've got unfinished business.

Her throat was suddenly very dry, and the temperature dropped what felt like twenty degrees in the span of a second. It really had been the poacher she had seen at the show. He knew where she worked. And it seemed like he had a score to settle.

"Well, at least he came to where you work and not where you live." Reese pointed out, trying to find a silver lining.

"That's really not comforting," Nikki grimaced, looking at the note. "I mean, I work here. I don't really want him to take his anger out on me." She glanced hurriedly over at KK. "Uh, you either, of course."

"Kotzbrocken," Pamela grumbled from her chair. "Er ist ein Backpfeifengesicht."

"English, please," Nikki sighed, folding her arms. "I can't understand all your fun insults if they're in German."

Pamela clicked her tongue. "The literal translation of the second part is that he is a person in need of a fist to the face."

"And the first bit?" KK asked.

Pamela scratched her chin. "There isn't really an English word for it," she mumbled. "Again, the literal translation is 'lump of puke.'"

Nikki, KK, Reese, and Pamela all laughed loudly, the merry sound echoing through the half-finished sanctuary where they were all relaxing. It was complete enough to lounge in. The bar was finished and stocked, and they had moved in some furniture. It was coming along quite nicely, and the glass dome overhead let warm late afternoon sunlight stream into the opening.

"It is disturbing," Reese shuddered, concerned. "Are you all right?"

"A bit shaken up," KK admitted. "Though, right now, it's nothing I can't handle." She looked at the fabric between her hands and the needle poking out where she had paused in her cross-stitch to chat.

Pamela was a cross-stitching freak. She was incredible at it, able to make intricate patterns in seemingly no time. She'd also been trying to convince Reese, Nikki and KK to join in for a year now with increasing fervor.

KK'd given into Pamela's request finally to try it, figuring that Reese and Nikki were right in their assertions that she needed a new hobby. Either in support or out of fear of being left out, Reese and Nikki had taken up the hobby as well. So all four of the women were cross-stitching together. KK's was fairly simple for her first time. She'd wanted to do something more advanced, but Pamela had dissuaded her from it, and based on how long it had taken her to get into the soothing rhythm of cross-stitch and figuring out how to follow a pattern involving three different colors, she had to admit Pamela had probably been right in her advice. She had picked a dolphin leaping into the air, with droplets of water spraying all around and the ocean beneath it. She hated to admit that Pamela had been right in getting her to pick a simpler one. Learning how to follow the pattern was harder than she'd imagined.

"You should go to the police," Nikki urged. "They can't ignore a threat like that."

KK snorted, jabbing the needle down into the next hole. "They're not going to do anything," she breathed. "Not with something this ambiguous."

The other women didn't respond, and an unsettling quiet filled the air. They knew she was right, but none of them liked the fact.

"I'll go if anything else happens," KK promised. "Until then, I don't really see a point."

"Any idea who it might be?" Pamela asked.

"I was telling Justin about it — one of the best parts of being in love is that you share everything," Nikki beamed. Pamela rolled her eyes and muttered something under her breath. "He says he's heard rumors of some guys holed up near some tourist traps near Lanikai beach."

"There's no way they'd be there," Reese said. "Too many people."

"Which would make them harder to find!"

"My bet is that they're here, closer to Marine World," KK asserted. "Based on where we found them."

"You don't think they might go hunting or whatever you want to call it further away from their hideout?"

"It's possible," KK admitted. "It's just a hunch. Especially since the poacher made an effort to come here and threaten me."

Again, that uncomfortable silence filled the room, laced with a small but noticeable tint of fear to it. None of the women wanted to think about the fact that KK had been threatened, or whether or not it might escalate.

"Let's talk about something more pleasant," KK finally suggested.

"Yeah, like athlete's foot," Nikki said.

"Or the fact that a bunch of new big shots from the mainland are buying up oceanfront property for private parties," Reese grumbled.

"Wait, seriously?" KK asked.

Reese nodded, her beautiful, dark face contorted in frustration. "They came to me first, actually," she explained. "They wanted a middleman here on the island so they didn't have to do the heavy lifting. When I found out what it was for, I said I wasn't going to help them, no matter how much they offered me." She glowered. "They ended up going with Evan Abrams."

"Isn't he your biggest competition?" KK asked.

"Yup. He actually called to gloat and 'thank me' for giving him the business." She sighed. "I don't regret saying no, but I am still pissed."

"I mean, more tourism isn't necessarily bad for the economy," KK pointed out. "But yeah, I hate the fact that they're making it harder for locals to buy property."

"Oh, I hope they don't try and make any of them wedding venues," Pamela said. "I don't think I could stand it if I had a couple who insisted on using one of those properties for their event. I prefer using locally owned spots whenever I can."

"We know," the other three women said in near-perfect unison.

"Just like you push Uncle Senior's malasadas on all your clients," KK said teasingly.

"Of course I do! They're phenomenal and perfect. And all the weddings I plan have to be perfect. Hence, his malasadas need to be included."

"I'm pretty sure you've made Uncle Senior a millionaire at this point," Reese said, laughing.

"My wedding was perfect," Nikki sang. "The dress, the fact that it rained a bit but not enough to ruin my makeup or make us have the wedding indoors. The food, the band…"

"You're welcome," Pamela quipped, arching an eyebrow in irritation.

"You're acting like I'm not giving you any credit!" Nikki pouted. "Don't you think I know all of it was down to you?"

Pamela softened a bit at the praise, but it was still obvious she was grumpy about the conversation.

The women continued talking, Reese sharing juicy gossip about some of their acquaintances on the island, and Nikki using every possible chance to bring up Justin or her wedding or love. Eventually, the wine came out, and everyone was in good spirits until the door to the sanctuary opened and Tony came in, his expression grim and almost stricken.

"What's wrong?" KK asked her pleasant buzz from the wine evaporating almost instantaneously. She glanced up at the glass dome. When had it gotten dark? "What are you doing here this late?"

"I was finishing cleaning," Tony started. It was a testament to how serious the situation was that he didn't complain about the workload. "I wanted to get ahead on it before the next show so I decided to work a bit late tonight. Anyway, I was out on the beach cleaning and..." He took a deep breath. "A dead dolphin washed up on shore. I thought you'd want to know."

There was a long silence as the women all processed the words. Anger boiled up inside KK as it sunk in. Another dolphin dead. After everything that had happened, the fact that the poachers were still out there at it again was nearly too much to bear.

"Now this is something to go to the police with," KK declared.

SEVEN

Chapter Seven

KK stormed up the steps of the police station before the sun had fully crested the horizon, that anger still sizzling in her veins. It hadn't subsided since last night. She stomped into the lobby and marched to the glass in front of the reception area. A man looked up, blinking in surprise, clearly taken aback by her ire.

"Can I help you?" he asked a little timidly.

"I want to talk to the chief," she demanded.

"Um, he's not in right now," he told her. "He usually doesn't get in for another hour."

"That's fine." She folded her arms. "I'm more than happy to wait."

"Can I have a name?"

She gave it to him, then went to the nearest chair and plopped down.

It was nearly two hours before the locked door to the rest of the station opened, and a large, clean-shaven man came out, glancing around until his eyes landed on the only person in the waiting room.

"Ms. Kawai?" he asked.

KK nodded and stood.

"I'm Chief James Knight," he stated. "Come on back."

She followed him back. The station was extensive, filled with both uniformed and plainclothes officers. Some of them watched with interest as she followed the chief. If she weren't so angry, she might have felt self-conscious about the attention. Right now she was too preoccupied with trying to get justice for the dead dolphin to really care what the other officers might think.

Chief Knight's office was spacious but looked surprisingly barren. There were photos of people who must have been his wife and kids on his desk and a closed filing cabinet in one corner. But the desk itself looked devoid of papers as if he had no work to do. Considering how busy this area of the island was, with all the tourists and businesses, she would have thought his desk would be overflowing with paperwork. Either he was incredibly efficient at his job and worked like a horse every day of the week, or he was lazy and did nothing. She wasn't sure which it was yet. "So what can I help you with?" he asked. His chair made a soft groaning sound as he reclined into it.

"A couple weeks ago I was attacked by poachers," she began.

"Oh yeah, I heard about that." He sighed and scratched his chin. "Hate to say it but I don't have any information. As soon as we do, one of my officers will—"

"That's not why I'm here," KK interrupted.

Knight's dark brown eyes narrowed as he studied KK, sweeping up and down her as if sizing up a potentially formidable opponent. He kicked his legs up on his desk, reclining even further.

"All right then," he drawled. "What is it?"

"A dolphin washed up on shore last night," she said.

He blinked, then his brow furrowed. "There are stranding networks and other people for that," he replied. "Call them. That really isn't a matter for the police."

Lazy, then, she thought, trying to keep her anger in check.

There was a knock on the open door, and KK turned to see Kremer's head sticking through the door frame. He blinked, bemused when he saw KK. "Miss Kawai?" he asked.

"This is the man you should be talking to," Knight said, gesturing at the detective. "He's the one in charge of the case, after all."

She gritted her teeth, stuffing her hand in her pocket and fishing out the note taped to her door. "What about this?" she asked, stuffing it in Knight's face.

He squinted, then shrugged. "Not much we can do."

"You could dust for fingerprints, do a handwriting analysis, anything, really," she exasperatedly suggested. "It's a threat."

"It's not even a death threat." Knight yawned. "And I'm not going to tie up department resources on a note like that."

"Sir," Kremer said after looking at the note KK had pushed into his hand. "This isn't something we should take lightly. I think it's serious, and almost certainly tied to the assault—"

"If she gets more, she can come back," Knight interrupted with a dismissive wave of his hand. "Now I'm a very busy man, so unless you have something important to tell me, I suggest you leave."

Fuming, KK stalked out of the station, not bothering to talk to Kremer. Her mind was reeling with anger and her body shook with anxiety. The police weren't going to do anything, not even about the threat she'd received. Kremer didn't seem too bad as a detective, but that didn't mean much when his boss refused to listen. She sighed and ran her fingers through her black hair, looking out at the crystal blue ocean, the sun glinting off it as it rose into the sky. Right now, she felt totally lost. And even if she wouldn't admit it, she was a little frightened. It was impossible to know what was going on or how best to handle it. It wasn't as though she had experience with poachers or any insight that might help her locate them.

She wanted to act, to get ahead of this, but the answer as to how to do so eluded her.

Her stomach growled loudly. Right. In all the excitement, she hadn't eaten yet. After a frustrating morning of dealing with the police and failing to get anything accomplished, as well as how stressed she was, there was really only one option for food.

Uncle Senior's malasada shop was packed this morning, filled with a mix of curious tourists and local regulars that created a line nearly to the door. KK's stomach growled even louder as the scent of freshly baked dough hit her nostrils and she had to force herself not to moan in excitement.

The line moved quickly, Uncle Senior's staff working seamlessly and effortlessly to move things along. KK watched as they replaced empty trays in the display cabinet with new ones filled with fresh goods.

When she finally got to the front, she was pleasantly surprised to see Uncle Senior himself stroll out of the back kitchen area. The man was older, his dark skin leathery and his once dark hair almost pure gray now. He broke into a warm smile when he saw KK.

"Good to see you!" Uncle Senior greeted, still beaming. His face fell a fraction when he saw KK's face. "Rough morning?"

"Something like that," KK admitted, sighing even as she gave a smile. "Just been a lot going on. Can I get a dozen? Assorted, but at least two of them pineapple?"

"I think we can manage that. And you know, I just so happened to have finished a fresh batch."

Five minutes later, KK walked out with a warm cardboard box of malasadas. Her stomach refused to wait until she got to Marine World, so she flipped it open. She frowned when she looked in the box, then smiled warmly.

Two extra malasadas were nestled snugly in the box.

She grabbed one hurriedly, and bit into it. It was still warm, and the pineapple filling burst into her mouth. She finished it in three large, quick bites.

At least some people are on my side, she thought, her mood instantly lifting as she plucked another from the box.

Eight

Chapter Eight

Unease began to creep into her thoughts again as she moved down the road. Uncle Senior's wasn't too far from Marine World, so it was easy to walk to whenever she got a craving for the treats. It was both a blessing and a curse. This morning she wished she had driven; she was certain that someone was watching her.

KK took a long, deep breath and forced herself not to turn around. She was probably being paranoid. There was no way she was actually being followed. That kind of stuff only happens in movies. If she turned around, she was just feeding that paranoia.

Even as she told herself that, she still felt eyes on her back, and it made her skin prickle. Finally, she couldn't help it, she turned as surreptitiously as she could, trying not to draw attention to the fact that she was looking behind her.

The crowd behind her was surprisingly large, grouped in their own clusters as they made their way to their destinations. None of them seemed to be paying her the least bit of attention, though.

She did a second take, this time looking closer, and her attention honed in on a man in a ball cap that was drawn down over the top half of his face. The bottom half was obscured in shadow, making it hard to pinpoint any identifiable features. Goosebumps crept up her skin as she looked at him.

Because the man looked an awful lot like the man from the audience yesterday.

She couldn't be certain, not from this distance and not with the cap, and she didn't want to get close enough to find out. She didn't know if the man was following her, but she had a sneaking suspicion her gut was right, and her gut was telling her to move as quickly as possible.

Every so often on the ten-minute walk from Uncle Senior's to Marine World, she would glance behind her, searching the crowd for the man in the hat. The first two times she did this, he was there. The third, he had vanished, as if he'd gone onto one of the side streets. That didn't stop her from continuing to glance around for him. He never showed up again, which somehow only made her more uneasy.

You're making things up, KK told herself as she looked one more time before unlocking and pushing open the doors to the employee's entrance at Marine World.

She put the malasadas in the break room for everyone else to enjoy, then strolled toward the changing room, her mind still racing with unpleasant thoughts. She needed to clear her head.

Minutes later, she had changed into her wetsuit and was climbing the metal stairs to the overhang on Jasper's tank. He was still separated from the others. Corey and Carey, who had been a duo their entire lives, might not take kindly to a newcomer. She would have to introduce them more slowly.

Jasper looked up at her, clicking hello. The clicks and chatters amplified, growing more excited when she dipped her feet into the water. He dove beneath the surface as she slipped into the tank. A moment later, he remerged right next to her, shooting air from his blow hole directly onto her.

KK laughed, smiling. "Hey buddy," she cooed, petting him on the head before swimming toward his favorite ball. "How are you doing today?"

Jasper chirruped back at her as if he were answering the question. His attention, however, was fixed on the ball in her hand, waiting eagerly for the play to begin. When she threw the ball, however, she overshot, and it landed outside of the tank and on the concrete floor, slowly rolling away. The calf turned to look at her, giving a look that could only be described as scolding.

"Sorry," KK sighed. "Been a bit of a rough day. My head isn't screwed on straight."

Jasper swam toward her, nuzzling against her to comfort her. His dark eyes looked up at her with concern as he chittered.

"I'll be alright," she whispered, stroking him gently. His skin was silky smooth and her fingers glided along it. "Things just need to simmer down a bit is all. This whole poacher thing really has me freaked out, and it's hard for me to know what to do, you know? I don't want any more animals to die and it feels like I'm on my own. Even if the Coast Guard tries and helps, it still feels like it's up to me."

There was a soft thump as something hit the water. She glanced up to see the white ball bouncing up and down with the movement of the ripples it had created.

"Everything okay?" Deborah asked as she came up to the metal stand. She was in her wet suit, but she sat cross-legged on the edge of the fake rocks that made up the overhang.

"Thanks for grabbing this. I didn't feel like getting out of the water yet. As for if everything is alright, that depends," KK answered, swimming toward the ball. "How much did you hear?"

"Enough to know you're worried," Deborah pointed out. KK tossed the ball to Jasper, who swam after it eagerly, before turning back to her employee. She was startled by the obvious concern on the petite woman's face, her almond eyes narrowed in worry. It was touching. Deborah didn't show it often, but she had a soft side to her that contrasted with her sometimes standoffish nature.

"Just frustrated," sighed KK. "Police won't help, and I called the coast guard earlier. They're too busy with other things to be of much use. And the Sanctuary is taking longer than it should to get open, and as much as I love Jasper he still hasn't really acclimated to anyone but me. Tim a little bit but not as much as I would like. It's just a lot."

"Things will come around," Deborah assured her. "And you've done really good work with Jasper. I'm sure it's only a matter of time before he gets used to the rest of us."

"You should try and train him a bit while I'm here," KK suggested. "Maybe that will help encourage him. I love the guy but he needs to learn to listen to you guys as well."

Deborah hesitates, but at the look on KK's face, her features soften a bit.

"Alright," she breathed.

KK clambered out of the water. Jasper followed after her, the white ball in his mouth, looking almost offended that she had cut their playtime short.

"Jasper," Deborah called, and Jasper turned to look at her. "Can you do some jumps for me?"

Deborah made the 'jump' gesture that KK had taught him. But instead of heading to the center of the tank and jumping into the air, he stayed exactly where he was, ball still in his mouth, staring at Deborah.

"Come on, please?" Deborah asked, making the motion again. "There's a fish in it for you if you do."

Again, Jasper just stared at her. He glanced over at KK who stayed motionless as she tried to let Deborah take control of the situation. Eventually, to her relief, he swam to the center of the tank and dove down. However, instead of jumping like he'd been asked, he simply stayed submerged, swimming contentedly, blatantly ignoring Deborah's repeated attempts to coax him into performing. It went on for a solid five minutes, during which Tim appeared and watched from the side of the tank, clearly biting his tongue and trying not to laugh.

"Maybe he's tired," KK said encouragingly, but she knew that wasn't it.

"Let Tim try," Deborah said, more than a little annoyed. "I've got to get ready for a class, anyway."

"Tim, you're up," KK said.

Tim nodded, then hopped up to the overhang. Jasper, who had reemerged and was currently playing with the ball, stopped and looked at Tim with a similar look that he had given Deborah.

"Hey, Jasper," Tim crooned. "Good to see you again. Let's show off your tail-walk."

It was a smart move. Tail-walking was Jasper's favorite trick. There was something about scooting across the water on his tail that he seemed to love. If he was going to listen to a command, that would be it.

At first, Jasper just stared at Tim. After Tim made a circular motion with his hands for the third time, Jasper finally listened, though not without a fair amount of what was unmistakably sass.

He's like a teenager, KK thought, and giggled.

Tim was at least more successful than Deborah, though that wasn't saying much. Jasper listened about a fifth of the time, and when he didn't feel like listening to Tim's commands, he simply swam and played with his ball and did as he pleased.

"Is that the new dolphin?" A slightly nasally, female voice called. KK closed her eyes in mild annoyance before turning to look at the newcomer, a stunning, dark-skinned woman with bright blue eyes.

"Hi Peggi," KK waved. "I didn't realize you were coming in today.

"I was in the area and wanted to see if Tim wanted to grab lunch," Peggi replied, yawning. She watched her boyfriend as he waved idly.

"I can take a break in a few minutes," he said. "Just let me finish his training session. Oh, and I need to get a picture. My followers love this little guy since he has such a great story."

Peggi smirked in part fondness, part exasperation at her boyfriend as he turned to continue working with

Jasper. "I heard that that dolphin is a real pain to work with."

KK turned wide eyes at Tim, who raised his hands rapidly.

"I said he was still getting acclimated," he insisted. "Nothing about him being a pain. I like him."

Jasper clicked, then rolled over several times, mistaking Tony's attempts at placating KK as a command.

"He's cute," Peggi cooed, walking up to the side of the tank and watching Jasper roll around. "I'm sorry about his fin. Is he getting better?"

KK was about to answer when Tony appeared. He was in his wetsuit, damp hair dripping into his face. Even KK couldn't deny the fact that there was something about a wetsuit that really, really suited him.

"How's the other rescue guy doing?" KK asked. They'd come across an emaciated dolphin trapped in a fisher's net a couple of months ago, and they had brought him to take care of him before releasing him back into the ocean. Since he'd only ever known ocean life, neither KK nor her parents thought he should stay longer than necessary.

"Pretty good," Tony surmised. "I think he'll be able to be released in a week or so, though we'll need to make sure he hasn't gotten too used to humans."

"We'll worry about that if it becomes an issue," KK stated. "In the meantime, I think he'll be alright."

"It must be sooo difficult taking care of dolphins like that," Peggi pouted, who'd been blatantly looking Tony up and down during the exchange. "I don't know how you do it."

If Tony even noticed the fluttering eyelashes or the 'come hither' look Peggi was giving him, he didn't acknowledge it. Instead, he just shrugged.

"It's hard work, and KK is definitely a slave driver." He winked at KK to show he was joking. "But it's worth it."

"I'll bet working with dolphins is a great workout," Peggi winked. "You look like you are in really good shape."

She can't be serious, KK thought. She glanced over at Tim, who didn't seem to notice at all that his long-term girlfriend was blatantly flirting with another guy right in front of him. It would be funny if it weren't also a bit bewildering.

But again, Tony seemed completely oblivious to the attention. "It's definitely kept me in shape," he agreed. "And working here is definitely the most fun I've ever had at a job."

As KK was debating whether or not to step in and save Tony from Peggi's blatant advances, Tim hopped down from the tank, phone in hand as he tapped the screen.

"I got some great photos. People are going to love it." He barely glanced up from his phone as he spoke. "Do you mind if I take off a bit early for lunch since Peggi's here?"

Peggi seemed to realize that her boyfriend was finished and stepped away from Tony and sauntered over to Tim, linking arms with him while doing her best to stay dry.

"Sure," KK replied. "If you bring something back, I'll pay you for it."

"On it."

When Tim and Peggi were gone, KK turned toward Tony. "Did you not see any of that?" she asked.

Tony blinked, head tilting as he pushed the damp hair plastered to his forehead away from his face. "See any of what?"

"Never mind."

"I actually came looking for you," he said. "I saw the malasadas in the kitchen and guessed you were the one that brought them. You only do that when you're in a really bad mood."

"You're not wrong," KK admitted, looking over at the tank. Jasper was swimming gracefully, but when he saw her looking at him, he stopped, swimming over to the glass and pressing his nose against it before swimming in lazy circles near where they were standing as if trying to be near her and give her some comfort.

"Well, I got some decent news this morning," Tony added. "When I reported the dead dolphin, I mentioned to the people who came to take care of it about the poachers. They actually had heard about it because the Coast Guard told them to keep an eye out. It sounds like the Coast Guard actually knows who one of them is. They haven't caught him yet, but it sounds at least like the investigation is moving forward."

KK let out a long sigh. It wasn't the best news it could be, but it wasn't terrible either. At least it was something. If they identified one, then there was a chance they could find out the rest.

"Right," she said, nodding briefly as she mulled it over. "It's a start, at least."

"Don't worry." Tony put a hand on her shoulder. "They'll catch the rest of them. I'm sure of it."

"They better." Her grin was almost feral. "Because If they don't, then I will."

Nine

Chapter Nine

She knew something was wrong when Nikki appeared in her office with a strange look on her face.

"What is it?" KK asked, a pit forming in her stomach. She knew Nikki well enough to know that the look on her face didn't mean anything good.

"Animal Control is here," Nikki declared, glancing back over her shoulder as if expecting them to be right behind her.

"Are they here about the rescue?" It wasn't uncommon for Animal Control to want to look in on the dolphins they were rehabilitating, especially if they were concerned that release would threaten the population.

"I don't think so," Nikki said quietly. "They said they wanted to check in on the calf."

The pit in her stomach swelled to the size of a boulder. "Why are they interested in Jasper?" she asked.

"I have no idea." Nikki looked over her shoulder again. "But they don't look as if they're in the mood to wait or deal with anyone other than you."

Not willing to waste any more time, KK stood and followed Nikki.

The two Animal Control personnel, a man of average height and a tall woman, were standing by Jasper's tank, studying him and murmuring to one another. Jasper, for his part, was watching them distrustfully as he lurked on the opposite side of the tank.

"Hi," KK said, smiling. "How can I help you?"

"I'm Jenna, and this is Pete." The tall woman with hair the same color as KK's shook her hand, before looking back at the tank. "We got word of a dangerous dolphin calf that's attacked some of your employees."

KK's mouth dropped to the floor. She looked over at Nikki, who looked just as dumbfounded as KK felt.

"No," said KK slowly. "Jasper hasn't attacked anyone. Can I ask who told you this?"

"An anonymous concerned citizen," Pete retorted. "We're here to assess how much of a danger he is."

"Jasper's a little ornery with people other than me, but he hasn't hurt anyone," KK objected. "The worst he's done is splash people. He hasn't hurt any of my team."

"We're just following up on what we heard," Jenna replied, not backing down.

"Well, no offense, but that's stupid," Nikki fumed, her eyes blazing furiously. "In fact, I'll prove it."

Without even bothering to change into her wet suit, Nikki marched up to the top of the tank and jumped into the water without hesitation. The two agents jumped, Jenna, taking a step toward the steps as if to pull Nikki out of the water.

KK watched, trying not to hold her breath. Jasper would never hurt Nikki, but if he behaved poorly, Animal Control might use that as an excuse to put him down.

Luckily, Jasper seemed to sense the importance of the moment, and he swam toward Nikki. He didn't nuzzle up against her like he would KK, but he did play with her, whistling happily as he circled her, balancing the ball on his nose and splashing her with his tail. The Animal Control watched on uneasily. Jenna's shoulders began to relax as she watched, but Pete still looked on with distaste.

"As you can see," Nikki proved, climbing out of the water. "Jasper's a sweetheart."

"Hmph," Pete said, scowling. "Well, just be aware that if we get any other complaints, then we'll be back."

"Next time, I'd appreciate it if you brought some evidence with you." KK folded her arms. "You don't have to tell me who it is, but if they can't show you a bite mark or a video of Jasper hurting someone, then I'm not letting you do anything to that adorable creature."

Unfortunately, or perhaps fortunately, Jasper chose that specific moment to come up to the side of the tank. He looked at them all and, before KK even realized what he was doing, his tail flew into the air and came slapping back down, slamming into the water. The water sprayed over the side of the tank and landed on the two Animal Control agents, soaking them almost entirely.

"I'm so sorry," KK gushed, holding her hand to her mouth as if mortified. In reality, she was just trying to hide the wide smile and laugh threatening to emerge. "That's just how he says hello."

Neither Pete nor Jenna looked particularly pleased at the greeting. Pete scowled.

"We'll be keeping an eye out," he grunted, and the two Animal Control agents marched off.

"You really know how to win people over, don't you?" KK asked Jasper when they were gone.

Jasper clicked happily, swimming in circles, clearly pleased with himself. It was impossible not to laugh.

"You're a mess," KK chuckled. Then she turned to Nikki. "Thanks for looking out for him."

"Of course. Besides, it's purely selfish. I want Jasper to like me, too." She winked at KK. "Now come on, Reese and Pamela are over in the Sanctuary. That's what I was coming to tell you before I got distracted by the Animal Control guys."

Nikki, looking down at her clothes that were clinging to her damp skin, quickly accepted the towel that KK had grabbed from the nearby cabinet. She toweled off as best she could before picking up a spare sweatshirt from her locker to hurry along with KK to meet their waiting friends.

Pamela and Reese were indeed in the sanctuary, lounging in two of the chairs and cross-stitching.

"Anyway, so you know that Alexis was dating Jonathan for years. Apparently, he started dating Crista behind her back. But Akoni, who's liked Alexis for a while now, found out…" Reese trailed off, cutting the gossip short when she saw the expressions on KK's and Nikki's faces. "Uh-oh."

"No kidding," KK sighed, walking over to the box where she was keeping the cross-stitching stuff. "Animal Control came to talk to us about Jasper."

"What?" Reese scoffed, at the same time Pamela exclaimed, "Was hast du gesagt?" in German.

"Yup," KK said bleakly. "Someone called Animal Control about him. No idea who or why."

"Who would do something like that?" Reese demanded.

"That's what I'm wondering, too," KK breathed. She glanced down at her cross stitch. So far, she was a little over a third of the way through. She had the dolphin's face and completed one of the colors of the water. She tried not to compare that to the fact that Pamela had completed two far more intricate and larger projects in that time. She was new to the craft, as was Nikki. Besides

Pamela, Reese was the only one who had experience before now.

She grabbed the small box of supplies, including the pattern and fabric and thread, and plopped it in front of her seat. Before she sat, she walked over to the bar. "Anyone want a glass of wine?" she asked.

Pamela and Nikki both raised their hands. When KK opened the cabinet to grab three stemless glasses, she paused. There was a note tucked in one of the glasses.

KK – Can you meet me at the beach tomorrow after dark? – Tony

"He could have just texted me," she muttered, stuffing the note into her jacket pocket and pouring the wine.

"Anyway," Reese continued after KK had sat down and grabbed her stitching supplies. "Did you guys hear about the drama between the owners of Bar City and The Cove? Apparently, they're having disagreements about property lines, and I just heard that Bar City's owner, Lawrence, tried to rat out The Cove and tell the authorities they don't have a liquor license, which just isn't true. And some of the Cove's employees and the owner, Akamu, decided to get back at him by throwing rotten fish into their kitchen."

"There's no way that's true," Nikki mused, eyes bright with the thrill of new gossip. "Justin works right next to there, he would have told me if something like that was going on."

"You'd be surprised what men will keep from their wives." Reese winked. "Just ask Pamela."

She nudged the older woman, who snorted in mock irritation, but there was definitely playfulness there.

"Yes, you would be surprised what Justin gets up to when he's not around," Pamela stated. At the stricken look on Nikki's face, Pamela laughed. "Nur ein Witz. Just a joke. Your husband is as devoted to you as you are him."

"I don't know. I don't think she's all that devoted," Reese mused. "How many times has she mentioned Justin this week?"

Nikki stuck out her tongue. The other two women laughed. KK, however, remained stoic, her mind still too fixated on Jasper and the mysterious arrival of the Animal Control agents.

"Hey, it's going to be okay," Nikki soothed, her hand reaching over to squeeze KK's shoulder. "We've taken care of them this time. We can do it again if they come back."

"I hope so," KK replied, but there was no confidence or determination in her voice, only raw anxiety that made her stomach do somersaults. She stared down at the cross stitch in her hand, the half-formed face of the dolphin staring back at her as her mind spun.

The next morning, KK found Tony cleaning the outdoor arena. He glanced up when he saw her and smiled.

"Here to give me more work?" he asked. "I already cleaned out the main tank and fed all the dolphins, including the one we're releasing tomorrow, and I got the boat and sling ready for transportation. I'm pretty sure I should qualify as employee of the year at this point. Where's my plaque?"

"Did you remember to change Jasper's diet today?" she asked. Tony bit his lips, looking around awkwardly, about as blatant a 'no' as he could give without saying it outright. "Let's hold off on that plaque, then. No, I was coming to tell you I can't get to the beach tonight. I thought I could, but I forgot I had dinner scheduled with my parents tonight. Sorry about that. I wanted to see what you wanted to talk about or if we needed to reschedule."

Tony paused, his brow furrowing and his lips turning into a bemused frown.

"Sorry," he apologized. "Um, what are you talking about?"

She frowned. "Your note?"

"What note?"

"The note you left in the sanctuary?" She drew it out like a question. As she said it and studied his face, she realized that he had absolutely no idea what she was talking about. He simply stared at her like she had corn for ears.

She still had it in the jacket she was wearing. She dug around in her pocket and pulled it out, handing it to him. Already, her stomach was churning and her heart rate spiked as the confused expression on Tony's face turned to concern.

"That isn't me," he confirmed, after reading it. "I wasn't even in the sanctuary yesterday, and that's not my handwriting."

"It's not?"

"Mine is way messier," he stated. "You should know that."

"It's not like I pay attention to your penmanship on a regular basis," she replied. "if it wasn't you, then who was it?"

Except she realized she already knew, and the thought made her sick with anxiety. According to the expression on Tony's face, he was thinking it, too. His eyes widened slightly.

"You don't think..."

He didn't need to finish. KK shrugged, trying and failing to make it look nonchalant. "I think it's the most reasonable conclusion," she stated, as she thought the same thing. "Even if I don't like what it means."

She didn't need to elaborate. There was really only one person who would be interested in luring her out to the beach late at night. Someone who had already proven he somehow knew how to break into Marine World. Someone who—and as the thought struck her so did a new burst of protective rage—had a grudge against an adorable dolphin, and might submit a fake call to Animal Control in petty revenge.

It seemed that the poachers weren't quite done with her yet.

Chapter Ten

"Great job, Jasper," KK praised as she watched him jump through hoop after hoop, catching the ball in his mouth each time she threw it. She crouched down toward the water and stroked him gently as he swam up to her. "Keep this up and you'll be in the big leagues in no time."

Jasper clicked repeatedly. Then looked at her with unmistakable worry on his face. He chattered softly.

"I'm all right," she assured him. "Just worried about the poachers. But we'll get them taken care of, right?"

Jasper squeaked, nuzzled against her hand once more, and then swam away. As KK stood to go check on the twins, a voice floated toward her, growing louder.

"All right guys, how's it going? I've been getting a lot of comments asking for an update on the injured calf we got in a while ago, so I figured I'd show you how our little guy is doing."

Tim appeared, holding the phone up above him as he spoke. His shoulders were straight back and he was giving that winning, influencer grin she sometimes saw on him.

"Oh here's my boss, KK," he introduced. "KK, say hi to everyone."

He turned the phone screen toward her where she could see he was live. Comments were flying along the bottom of the screen, ranging from "YAY DOLPHINS" to "oh hey she's cute." She forced herself not to roll her eyes while Tim was live.

"Hey, everyone," she faltered, very aware of her damp hair and wetsuit and how she probably looked like a hot mess, regardless of what the comments were saying.

Tim wrapped his arm around KK, still grinning broadly. "Guys I've been trying to tell KK that we need a Marine World Instagram and TikTok, but she doesn't think anyone would be interested, so go ahead and tell her your thoughts and maybe we can convince her."

Instantly all the comments changed to "OMG YESSSSSSS" and "would totally follow" sprinkled with the occasional "it might be interesting" and "yawn."

"I'll think about it," KK demurred. She nudged Tim's foot in a silent, "finish your stream" command.

"Anyway, here's Jasper again." He turned to the tank where Jasper was watching curiously. The instant the camera turned toward him, Jasper immediately began to show off, almost as if he knew exactly what was happening. KK's mouth nearly dropped open at the sight. It was the most outgoing Jasper had been since he'd gotten here.

Tim explained how Jasper was doing to his audience, and Jasper even listened to some of the commands Tim gave him for tricks while KK watched on with fondness and amazement. Finally, Tim signed off and tucked his phone into his wetsuit.

"See?" he said, grinning. "I told you people love this place. And thanks for letting me do that."

"Next time maybe ask permission so I have some autonomy in the decision," suggested KK. "I would have told you to go ahead, you know, but it's at least nice to have the option."

"Sorry," he lilted, then quickly asked, "How are you doing, though? Tony told me about the note."

She hesitated for a moment. She'd always been taught to keep up a front around the employees. Not icing them out, but not letting them see if something is really bothering her. Considering how close she was with Nikki and Tony, she'd never done a particularly good job of listening to that point. But she didn't want any of them to worry about what was happening. But they also deserved to know.

"I've been better," she admitted. "The whole thing has been freaking me out a bit. I'm worried that all of this is going to hurt you guys or the dolphins, and that makes me feel guilty. You guys shouldn't have to deal with it as well."

"Guilty?" Tim stared incredulously. "You saved a dolphin from dying and stopped a poacher and you feel guilty? No offense, but you should get your head examined. You did a good thing and everyone here knows it and respects you for it. Seriously. I don't know of anyone who would be mad at you, but I promise no one at Marine World thinks less of you for getting threatened. And also don't think for a second that we won't step in and help if things get worse."

"Thanks." It was times like this that she remembered why she hired Tim. He was a good guy who loved animals as much as she did, even if he was a little too obsessed with his phone. But when he put it away and showed his true self, it was impossible not to like him. But she also didn't want to talk about it anymore. "How are you doing? How's Peggi?"

"Peggi's great. Busy with a shoot and she says she's going to the mainland in a couple of weeks." His eyes lit up. "Did I tell you I'm looking at getting a dog? I used to have one, but she died before I moved here. I love Peggi but I miss that animal companionship."

"You didn't tell me!" She clapped her hands eagerly. "Do you have one picked out?"

"Yeah." He fished his phone out again and clicked through a few pages before turning it to show an adorable blue merl puppy with pointy ears looking at the camera with chocolate-colored eyes. "She's technically a mix but she's mostly Australian cattle dog. Her name is Ginny."

"She's so cute," KK cooed. "If you do get her and don't bring her in, you're fired, by the way."

He chuckled. "I'll keep that in mind," he promised.

"What are you guys looking at?" Deborah asked as she walked up.

"Tim's looking at dogs," KK responded.

"For Instagram or TikTok?" Deborah joked as she looked at the photo.

"Hey, studies show that cute pets boost social media engagement by nearly fifty percent. She'll pay for herself in no time. Why do you think I film here all the time?" Tim shrugged, trying to be nonchalant.

KK knew the real reason he filmed here was because he was trying to raise awareness and he enjoyed making content. But she also knew that he was never going to open up to someone and be honest unless he knew them well or they dragged it out of him. For whatever reason, he liked to pretend to most people that his social media presence was all he cared about. The one time she'd tried to ask him about it, he'd said he had no idea what she was talking about, then went to talk about follower engagement for twenty minutes. She'd never asked him about it again.

"Come on," KK said, trying to avoid making things more contentious. "Deborah, mind working with Jasper for a bit? I want to see if he's had any breakthroughs after yesterday. You too, Tim."

They nodded. KK watched from the ground, trying to be as unobtrusive as possible so as not to influence Jasper too much. He was making improvements. He listened to Tim about half the time, and after splashing her a few times and pointedly ignoring her, he began to do the same for Deborah. It wasn't perfect, but it was still a blatant improvement.

All of a sudden there was a loud scream. All three of their heads snapped around in the direction it had come from. Even Jasper swam toward that side of his tank, curious as to what happened.

"That's Nikki," KK gasped with realization. Without waiting for the others to react, she ran in the direction of the shriek. Her stomach grew heavy with dread and her mouth was dry with fear. If something had happened to Nikki…

Deborah and Tim were hot on her heels, and the three of them skidded to a halt when they saw Nikki in Carey and Corey's tank, fully clothed. She was desperately trying to nudge Carey through the hole that led to one of the other tanks. It took KK a minute to realize the reason Nikki was so desperately trying to move the dolphin was because the water in the tank was dropping at an alarming rate. A moment later, she saw the reason.

There was a massive leak in the bottom of the tank, and water was beginning to pool on the concrete floor.

Not bothering to investigate the source of the leak, only recognizing that it was there, KK sprang into action, climbing up the ladder to the tank.

"Tim, get the poles, Deborah, make sure the other side of the tunnel is open and then close it as soon as we get Carey and Corey into that tank," KK directed as she hopped into the receding water next to Nikki.

They sprung into action, trying to work quickly before the water dropped too fast and stranded the twins. Once KK was able to coax Corey into the tunnel, the poles she'd ordered Tim to grab, ones with loops on them designed to help get the dolphins where they needed to go when they were being stubborn, went unused as Carey followed her brother into the tunnel and swam into the other tank. Nikki and KK slammed the door to the tunnel shut on their side.

"That was close," KK exclaimed, breathing heavily as she looked around. The water had nearly hit below the tunnel, which would have made it impossible to transfer the twins, and it was still dropping. With the tunnel door closed, the twins were safe. "Let's get out of here before it gets impossible for us to get out."

They clambered out of the tank. Tim was already bending and examining where the water was coming from. "It's a nasty crack," he observed, pointing to where water was spitting out of a break in the glass.

"How is that even possible?" KK asked. "That tank is new and do you know how much force it takes to crack the tank enough for it to leak out like that?"

"Not just that," Tim added. "Crack it enough for it to leak out but not enough for the tank to break entirely, which would have made a lot more noise."

He looked pointedly at KK.

"You think it was sabotage," she said, her voice hoarse.

"I think that's a possibility," Tim nodded.

"What happened, Nikki?" KK turned to look at her friend, who looked the most shaken out of any of them.

"I had just finished their training session for the day," she explained. "I was only coming back because I'd forgotten my phone. I was gone maybe five minutes. By the time I got back, there was already a lot of water on the floor and Carey and Corey were freaking out. I didn't give myself time to think, I just jumped in.

"And you wouldn't have walked back this way any time soon if you hadn't forgotten your phone," KK said. It was a statement, not a question. "Which meant that the tank could have emptied entirely before any of us noticed. Which means..." she trailed off, unable to say it.

"Which means that Corey and Carey might not have made it," Tim finished for her.

There was an unpleasant hush. The shivers racing along KK's body were because of the wetsuit, not because of any apprehension on her part. At least that's what she kept telling herself.

They mopped up the water as best as they could. They would need to get someone to come out and look at the tank, but KK could already tell that the damage was done. The tank, which had been Corey and Carey's main home, would be out of commission for a while. Luckily the spare tank had plenty of room, and the main thing was that they were alive.

"I've got to go call our repair guy," KK told the others, running her hand through her hair. She was suddenly very tired. All she wanted to do was sleep. It felt like things were piling up and she was beginning to feel overwhelmed.

But that was nothing to what happened when she got in her office and saw her office phone blinking, telling her she had a voicemail. She picked up the receiver and dialed her voicemail. After the robotic voice told her she had 'one new message,' it clicked over, and her blood ran cold.

"I hope those dolphins died," a gravelly voice that she had never heard before snarled. "Either way, you'll be seeing me soon. You and I have some unfinished business."

Eleven

Chapter Eleven

Her hands were still shaking as she sat at her desk when Tim strolled in.

"Hey, KK, Tony says he thinks he can fix it himself, but we'll need to order the new glass—" He cut himself off when he saw KK's reaction, the smile slipping from his face. He closed the office door behind him and hurried over. "What's wrong?"

Instead of answering, KK held out the receiver. Tim took it and placed it against his ear as KK replayed the message. His normally handsome features blanched as he listened, his eyes widening.

"Oh, wow," he muttered. "That's...uh..."

"Yeah." She took the receiver back from him and rubbed her face. "Not exactly how I was hoping today would go, you know?"

"I can't really blame you," he agreed. His hand went reassuringly to her shoulder. "There's a lot going on, and this guy isn't helping. But it's going to be alright, okay?"

"But what if it isn't?" She hated how small her voice sounded, how frightened. "I know that's the poacher. He all but admitted to sabotaging the tank—"

"But he didn't know it failed," he stated. "He's not here all the time. He broke the tank, then ran as quickly as possible."

"He knows how to get into the aquarium and the Sanctuary," she fretted.

"And we'll figure out how," Tim promised. "I know you're freaked out, but you're not alone. You've got me and Tony and Deborah and Nikki. We all love this place and we aren't about to let some jerk come in and ruin it for us."

She took a long, shaky breath, trying to command her hands to stop trembling with limited success. She forced herself to smile. "Thanks."

"Anytime." He gave her a quick, reassuring hug as she stood. "I think we should call the police, though. This stuff is serious. And it's something they can actually do something about."

She hesitated, biting her lip. She knew he had a point, but the thought of trusting the police after her last interaction was not an appealing one. "I don't know," she murmured.

"They'll be able to help better than anyone else," he pointed out. "And we have proof. They can't ignore the voicemail or the tank."

She chewed the inside of her lip as she considered. Finally, she nodded.

"Worth a shot."

"So what makes you think that this was vandalism?" Officer Charlie Akamai asked as he studied the large crack in the tank. His uniform shoes were soaked. Tim and Nikki were still trying to soak up the excess water. But it had been delayed by Nikki insisting on texting Justin what happened and by Tim deciding the incident was perfect content for a TikTok and taking five minutes to film a quick video—it was up to ten thousand likes in just over two hours, according to him—so the water still stood an inch high on the concrete floor in some places.

"I feel like it's fairly obvious," KK folded her arm. "None of my employees are going to intentionally destroy any piece of equipment, especially when it might harm one of the dolphins. And you don't get that kind of break naturally in glass."

"Hmm..." Officer Akamai scratched the dark stubble on his chin, glancing over at his partner, who was wandering around the area. "Sure, but is there any proof?"

KK bristled, and it was all she could do not to spit vitriol at them. "What else would it be?" She demanded through clenched teeth.

If Akamai or his partner, a guy named Shane Likeke, noticed her obvious irritation, they didn't show it. They continued wandering around the space, taking a couple of photos and notes.

"You said there was a voicemail?" Officer Likeke asked.

KK nodded. "The creep effectively confesses that he tried to kill the dolphins," she declared.

The two officers looked at one another, and frustration bubbled up in her stomach. That look told her they would rather be anywhere than right here, listening to her yammer on.

"Why don't you show us, then?" Officer Likeke said.

"Where is Detective Kremer?" KK asked as she led them to her office. "I'd hoped he would be here since it's his case."

"This isn't his case," Officer Akamai corrected, a little self-importantly. "He's dealing with your assault case. There's no evidence that the two are connected."

KK bit her tongue and instead focused on her steps to avoid saying anything she would regret later.

When they got to the office, KK dialed her voicemail and kept it on speaker. Her stomach was twisting itself into pretzels at the thought of having to hear that menacing, gravelly voice again. She didn't like thinking about the threat or what it might mean for the aquarium. She didn't want to have that reminder that someone was out there and had a grudge, and she didn't even know his name. She clicked over to her saved messages and held her breath.

"You have no saved messages."

The monotone declaration seemed to scream. The phone clicked off, but all KK could do was stare in disbelief.

The voicemail was gone.

"It was there," she insisted.

"Uh-huh," Akamai said, drawing out the word as if talking to a five-year-old. He glanced over at Likeke with a look that clearly translated to, this lady is nuts.

"I swear it was there," KK stammered. Her hand darted out and she jabbed each number to dial the voicemail with far more force than was necessary.

"You have no saved messages." The phone announced.

She went through every option on the voicemail menu, trying to pull up the menacing message again. But it was nowhere to be found. She took a step back, eyes wide.

"Someone erased the message," she insisted. She hurried over to the office door, examining the lock to see if there was any damage to it. There was nothing. Had she locked it? She couldn't remember. Her mind was spinning as everything moved in and out of her mind. There was only one person who might delete that message, and that was the man who'd sent it, the poacher. What if the guy was still here? He knew how to get into her office and he had already tried destroying one of her tanks. What if it didn't stop? What if he went and destroyed the rest of the tanks?

She looked back at the two officers to see them staring at her like she had two heads. She took a deep breath and tried to compose herself.

"It was there," she insisted. "Ask Tim. He heard it, too."

"We can't go around on a wild goose chase," Akamai sighed. "Right now that's all this is. Since we don't have the voicemail, we can't just go off the word of your employee." He yawned and straightened, walking past her out of the office. "We've seen enough."

KK huffed, trying to keep her cool as her anger boiled just beneath the surface. "Can I at least have a copy of the police report or a number I can give to my insurance?" she asked.

The two officers looked at one another with identical expressions of frustration. But Likeke nodded, scribbled some information on a sheet of paper, and handed it over to her.

"Feel free to reach out if you come up with actual evidence. Otherwise, there isn't really anything for us to go on," Likeke said before he and the other officer turned to walk away.

"You mean do your job for you?" KK mumbled, soft enough so that they couldn't hear. She sighed and started heading back toward the tank, wanting to confirm with Tim that the voicemail really hadn't been her imagination, when another familiar face brought a new round of dread and unease.

Normally, KK liked visiting with Rosie. But the grim expression on the activist's pretty round face didn't bode well.

"What is it?" KK asked.

"Um." Rosie hesitated, then plowed on. "Animal Control contacted me. They said there was an aggressive dolphin calf here and they wanted me to assess the threat."

"What?" KK gaped. "Jasper?"

"According to one of the agents, the calf tried to drown him," Rosie told her.

"Drown?! Jasper splashed water on them. That doesn't count as drowning."

"Ah." Rosie nodded as if everything made sense now. "I see. Well, they asked me to come take a look, so I said I would. I figured you would rather have me come than anyone else."

"You're not wrong there," KK sighed. "All right, let's get this over with."

Jasper was still pressed against the glass on the side of the tank closest to where the drama had happened earlier in the day. He saw KK and clicked agitatedly, his dark, intelligent eyes filled with worry and concern. His tail flicked back and forth in the water.

"Everyone's all right, Bud," KK soothed. Jasper seemed to relax at the words as if he understood them. "You remember Rosie? She's here to see how you're doing."

Rosie watched while KK led Jasper through some of the tricks they'd been practicing. He was a perfect gentleman, and Rosie watched on with a smile on her face the entire time.

"Well?" KK asked maybe thirty minutes later. "Does this seem like drowning behavior?"

Chuckling, Rosie shook her head. Then she sobered. "I'm on your side on this one," she promised. "And I'll tell Animal Control they're way off the mark. But I can only do so much. If you give them any excuse whatsoever, they'll find a way to either shut you down or euthanize him. Which reminds me, one of the officers wanted me to pass on the message that you need to keep your tanks up to code, otherwise they'll shut the whole thing down."

KK groaned and rubbed her temples. The headache was fighting with the anger rising again.

"That's just what I need today," she sighed. "Thanks for your help, Rosie."

"Of course." Rosie gave her a reassuring pat. "I've got to get going, but I'll give a glowing report to Animal Control. And if they keep bothering you, let me know. All right?"

KK nodded, but it was hard for her to say anything because a lump had formed in her throat. Rosie left with a wave, leaving KK and Jasper alone with their thoughts.

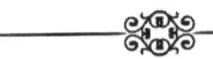

"You all right, KK?" Katerina asked. "You've been really quiet all night."

It was later that evening, and KK was over at her parent's house. She'd had dinner plans with them for a week. She would have canceled, but she also knew that would be a screaming red flag to her parents, and she was trying to pretend like everything was fine, even as she was fuming internally. She probably should have just told them she was sick.

"Just dealing with some problems at work," KK muttered, trying to sound nonchalant.

"Balancing the books?" her dad asked. "If they're off, you might be forgetting the cleaning supplies purchases. I always did. Or, if Carey is giving you trouble, just remember to give her an extra fish or two. But only when Corey isn't looking, because then he'll get jealous and—"

"Dad, business advice," KK groaned.

He frowned, scratching his chin. "Was I?" he asked Katerina.

"Yes, you were," Katerina pointed out. "And I don't think she's forgotten the cleaning supply purchases. What's wrong?"

For a moment, she thought about keeping it to herself. A paranoid part of her screamed that if she told them the truth, they would think she was a failure, and she didn't want that. But with all the stress in her life, she didn't think she could contain it, and the words came flowing out. She told them about her problems with Jasper and how Animal Control was acting weird. She told them how things kept being off around the aquarium. It didn't take long to tell, but when she was finished, it felt like the world had been lifted from her shoulders.

"I'm so sorry, sweetie," Katerina said sympathetically. She walked over and embraced her daughter. "I know how hard that can be."

"I remember how Simon was a handful," her dad recalled. "Think the only thing that calmed him down was mating Majestique."

"Yeah, but did Animal Control ever come and try to put either of them down?" Kat muttered. Her father didn't answer. "I don't know how to prove he's harmless. And I don't know who is telling them he's dangerous. None of it makes sense. And he's being difficult with everyone but me. He likes Tim a bit, but if we can't get him to be a bit more easygoing, I don't know what we'll do.

"Don't worry, sweetie," Katerina soothed. "That dolphin is a smart one. If you ask me, I think he's going to be an even better performer than Majestique."

"Really?" KK asked.

Katerina nodded. "You remember Koda? I always said he was the best performer we ever had. Jasper reminds me a lot of him. You might have been too young to realize it, but that dolphin had so much sass. But he absolutely adored your father."

Joseph nodded, taking a swig of beer. "I've worked with a lot of dolphins," he reminisced. "Koda was probably my favorite. And yeah, I think your mother is right when she says Jasper is a lot like him. I think if you keep with it and keep training him, he's going to be a star."

KK sighed, her breath shakier than she wanted to admit. Hearing her parent's conviction reassured her more than anything else.

"You got this," her dad winked. "If you didn't, we wouldn't have let you take over."

She smiled, even more of her worry and concern ebbing. "Thanks." She glanced down at her phone. "I've got to get going. I'll talk to you guys later."

The air was pleasantly warm when she stepped out of her parent's house and walked toward her car. An old sedan sat about halfway down the street. She wouldn't have paid it any mind if she hadn't seen its headlights blare on in her rearview moments after she pulled out of the driveway.

Her shoulders stiffened and her breath caught. She tried to keep her eyes on the road, but her gaze kept moving to the rearview. It was dark, so it was hard to tell, but she was certain that the sedan was following her. At the very least, a pair of headlights kept an even pace behind her, always the same distance back.

You're imagining it, she told herself. But it was impossible to believe it.

It was only a ten-minute drive from her parent's house to hers. But she wasn't about to drive near home if someone was following her. She made a right where she normally would have taken a left, and kept driving, regularly looking in the rearview.

And then the headlights were gone. No car on the road, nothing to indicate there ever had been one. She kept driving for another few minutes without purpose before finally heading home. There was no one following her.

However, that didn't stop her from looking up and down her own street several times before hurrying out of her car, running inside, and locking the door behind her.

Chapter Twelve

"And flip!"

Jasper, Corey, and Carey all jumped backward simultaneously, creating a tremendous splash that sprayed water over the first three rows of empty concrete seats.

"And one more time."

Again, the three dolphins obeyed KK in perfect unison, as if they'd been doing it for years. KK broke into what was quite possibly the biggest smile she'd ever had on her face.

"Great job, guys," she praised. "Really fantastic."

The dolphins all swam up to her, clicking and whistling as she bent down to grab fish from the bucket, tossing each of them one a piece.

"That's the best they've ever done," Tony boomed. "I honestly can't believe it. Weren't Corey and Carey antagonizing Jasper just a couple of days ago?"

"You know, it was the weirdest thing," KK said, stroking Jasper and Carey as they came up for pets. "When the twins' tank broke, we had to put them in with Jasper for a bit of time. I thought we were going to have to find a way to separate them, but they started getting along."

"Any idea why?"

KK shrugged. "Absolutely no idea," she confessed. "But I'm not going to look a gift dolphin in the mouth."

It felt like a miracle. She'd been training Jasper by himself but hadn't been able to get him and the twins to get along for more than an hour, and she'd been so worried about it that she'd been considering delaying Jasper's debut in the show, despite his natural showmanship. But when she'd come in the day after Rosie left and seen the three dolphins playing together and getting along, she decided to try and train all three of them together again. The change was miraculous. Today was the final dress rehearsal before the show tomorrow. It had been like the three of them had worked together for years. She couldn't have dreamed it better herself.

Tony snorted. "There was something else about the show," he recalled. "Did you notice that the twins were sort of taking Jasper's lead?"

KK glanced down at the dolphins, all swimming contentedly, as she considered this. "Yeah," she whispered.

"They definitely deferred to him a few times. I don't know why."

"Well hey, if it works, it works," Tony shrugged with a bold smile.

"How are the tank repairs going, by the way?" she asked, hopping down from the tank.

"Glass is on the way," he confirmed. "Should be here tomorrow or the day after, and I can finish that one. I've also been going through the other tanks and other gear, making sure it's up to code in case Animal Control decides to come around and mess things up again."

"You're a saint, Tony," KK remarked, sighing. "Thanks."

"It's what you pay me for," he said cheerfully. "I mean, if you want to pay me for doing nothing, I'd also be really happy with that, so that's definitely something we can talk about."

KK rolled her eyes. "Ask me when we don't have a gajillion things to do," she muttered.

"Hey, KK," Tim hurried over. He was soaked from his final trick with Jasper, one that the two of them had been working on together for a while now. At some point, Jasper had taken a shine to Tim, and he was the only trainer the young dolphin would listen to on a regular basis besides KK.

"That trick is amazing," KK said, grinning. "It's going to be a showstopper."

"Of course it is." Tim flashed his cock-sure grin. "It involves me." He gave a roguish wink. He pulled out his phone. "Any chance I could get a video of the three of them doing one of their tricks?" he asked. "It would be great for content."

"Considering the show is supposed to be a treat for guests and not for your followers, I'm going to say 'no.'" KK replied. When Tim opened his mouth to argue, she held up her hand. "Ask me tomorrow after we see how the show goes. You might catch me in a good mood."

"How about letting Peggi film the show?" he suggested.

She stroked her chin thoughtfully. "Will you clean out the dolphin tanks for a week? And I don't mean asking Tony to clean them for you." Off to the side, Tony pumped his fist excitedly, clearly thrilled at the idea of not having to clean the tanks for a while.

"Deal." Tim stuck out his hand and they shook.

"I still can't believe you wouldn't let him post photos of the broken tank on his socials," Peggi interjected, seemingly materializing from nowhere and linking arms with Tim. KK had absolutely no idea where she had come from. "It would have been such good content."

"I don't particularly like the idea of one of my employees capitalizing on problems happening at the aquarium." KK folded her arms as she stared down Peggi. "It sets a bad precedent and I find it distasteful."

Peggi's eyes narrowed and she opened her mouth to argue.

"Leave it, Pegs," Tim cautioned, typing away on his phone and not even looking at her. "She's got a point. And besides, with Animal Control breathing down our necks, I didn't want to post something like that."

Before Peggi said anything else, Nikki hurried in from the side, grinning widely.

"KK, great news!" she bubbled. Then she stopped when she saw Tim and Peggi. "Oh my god, you two are too cute," she squealed.

"We try." Tim gave his lazy grin as he glanced affectionately at his girlfriend.

"Soooo when are you two getting married?" Nikki asked in a sing-song voice. "You're around here all the time, surely it's come up."

"We've talked about it," Peggi shrugged. "We're waiting until we have a better idea of where we're going to end up. Neither of us are in any hurry."

"You should be," Nikki sighed. "It's so much better than dating. You have no idea."

Nikki was going into her normal spiel, one that she'd given the very single KK three times now, while Peggi stood there awkwardly, clearly trapped in the conversation. Tony was biting his lips behind Nikki's back, even as his shoulders shook in silent, amused laughter. KK forced herself not to look at him, because she knew she would collapse into giggles if they made eye contact.

Finally deciding to take mercy on the cornered Peggi, KK interrupted. "You said you had some good news?"

"Huh? Oh, yeah!" Nikki spun back toward KK, her marriage crusade temporarily forgotten. "The general contractor was trying to find you but I said you were busy. Anyway, he wanted me to tell you that they finished the final bits of the sanctuary. He said for you to take a look and let him know if there are any changes you want. When you give the thumbs up, he'll send the final invoice."

"That's great! Tim, Tony, can you put up the dolphins?"

"On it," Tony yelled after her.

They stepped inside the sanctuary and KK beamed. It still needed work. None of the plants for the garden or the water for the koi pond were in yet, but the foundations were all there. The stone floor that would be covered in moss looked natural as if it had been there for a thousand years. She could see where all the infrastructure was supposed to go. And for the first time, she really saw her vision coming to life.

"It's perfect," she breathed, grinning like a maniac.

"It's going to be amazing," Nikki agreed. "You're not going to get anyone to go to work if they have a breakroom like this."

"I'll have to make some calls to tell the next group they can come in and start with the landscaping," KK mused as she strolled around the perimeter. For fun, she hopped into the circular ditch that encased the middle sitting area, the ditch that would soon be filled with water for fish, and walked around once, before hopping out again. "But the GC is ahead of schedule, which is great. That guy is getting a massive bonus."

"I can't wait!" Nikki squealed, embracing her friend. "Oh, just wait until Justin hears about this. You know, I'll bet this place would be an amazing wedding venue. You should consider offering it up. Pamela would love it, and I'll bet you'd make bank."

"I'll consider it," KK said, smirking and trying to contain her amusement. "For now, let's just get it finished. Come on, I wanted to talk to Tim about that trick with Jasper."

They strolled out, jabbering with wide smiles on their faces. But all that good cheer evaporated when Tony approached them on their way back.

"Um, something is up with Jasper," he told her. KK's stomach plummeted. "He's acting weird."

"Show me."

Jasper was still in the outdoor arena, swimming back and forth agitatedly, slamming his tail against the glass as if trying to break out. He clicked and whistled angrily, thrashing in the water in a way that KK had never seen him behave before.

"Jasper, buddy, it's me," KK called out, running up to the side of the tank where Jasper was nearest. "What's wrong?"

Jasper didn't even look at her. Instead, he swam away a little, as if trying to look past her at something. She kept trying to get his attention, her confusion growing more and more as the dolphin continued to ignore her.

Then there was a loud clanging sound from inside. Jasper's movements grew even more wild and erratic at the sound and he chittered angrily.

"Tim, can you try and get him under control?" KK asked Tim, who was watching with Peggi nearby.

"Yeah, absolutely."

KK ran toward the sound, throwing open the door and rushing inside. She was near the rescue tank, where until recently, their foster dolphin had lived before they'd released them. A figure was on the overhang, his back to her as he hunched over. He hadn't noticed her. He was holding a giant tub of something, and although she couldn't see what it was, or what exactly he was doing, she could hear the sound of something being poured into the water, and the acrid smell of chlorine stung her nostrils.

When the figure turned to the side to cough, she recognized him instantly. It was the poacher.

He was pouring bleach into the dolphin tanks.

Chapter Thirteen

For a moment, all she could do was stand and stare in shock. Then red covered her vision and her entire body began trembling with undiluted rage.

He was trying to kill her dolphins.

She was going to make him pay.

She had enough hold of her senses to try and remain quiet as she crept toward the steps to the tank. Her eyes darted all around as she looked for some sort of weapon.

The man grunted, and KK froze. He stood, grabbed the bottle of chlorine, and walked down the metal steps. She stepped into the shadows, hoping that he hadn't seen her. He hadn't, and he walked past her, heading toward the next tank. Her eyes widened. He was wearing a Marine World wetsuit. That was how he had been able to get around without being noticed. As long as he stayed out of the way of the normal employees, no one would have questioned him. It wasn't unusual to have temporary help in the building during the week of a show so the trainers could focus more on training than cleaning.

She crept behind him. As she did, her hand reached out, grabbing a long metal pool net.

He stalked up the metal steps to the indoor training tank and crouched on the overhang and began fiddling with the bottle of bleach.

While he was twisting the cap, KK rushed up the steps. Using the pool net, she knocked the bottle of bleach out of his hand and away from the tank. It flew over the side and slammed onto the concrete floor.

"Don't. Hurt. My. Dolphins!" she yelled, accentuating each word with a whack from the pool net. But on the last word, the poacher grabbed the metal rod and yanked, jerking her off balance. KK stumbled, falling toward him. She tripped and slammed into the metal grating of the overhang.

Strong, meaty hands grabbed the collar of her wetsuit and dragged her over to the water. Before she could do anything to stop it, the poacher shoved her head below the surface.

One hand kept a grasp of her neck, and the other went to her head, locking it below the water. She thrashed and kicked, trying to make sure not to scream and fill her lungs with water. Her hands clawed at his arms, but his stolen wetsuit made it virtually useless. Her nails just scrabbled futilely against the thick slippery fabric.

Her heart began to race as her mind started panicking. She couldn't breathe. Her body begged her to move, to open her mouth and take deep lungfuls of air that weren't actually there. Her chest burned and her eyes began to sting. She tried to pull herself out from under him, but all of her motions were useless.

She was going to die. Drowned in one of her own dolphin tanks.

The thought was enough to give her a second wind.

She forced herself to go limp, to make it seem as though she were giving up or about to die. It was nearly impossible to go against her instincts and not fight, knowing she would die if she didn't get out of this situation, but it was her only option.

The grip the man had on her relaxed, and she made her move. She dove, kicking furiously and trying to get as far away from the man as possible. Her body was screaming for oxygen, but she couldn't resurface, not until she was far enough away that he couldn't get his hands on her.

She swam away from the overhang and finally resurfaced. She took deep, grateful breaths, gasping as the air flew into her lungs. But she didn't have time to savor it. Her head swiveled toward the overhang, where the man stood, glowering at her as she was safely out of reach in the middle of the tank.

"You think that's going to be enough?" he snarled.

It was the first time she had truly gotten a good look at his face and this close. His stubble was graying, but still mostly an ashy brown. His jaw was square, and his eyes were harsh and hazel, his skin tanned from being out on the water for hours on end. The end of a tattoo peeked out from beneath the stolen wetsuit.

"You're not going to hurt my dolphins," KK sputtered, but the fact that she was still gasping for breath made it a lot less intimidating. "Leave us alone before I call the police."

The fact that she was treading water and her only way out of the tank was through the poacher who had almost killed her made the threat laughably hollow. The man knew it, and he laughed.

"You think they're going to help you?" he asked. "Or Animal Control? Especially when they know how dangerous that calf of yours is?"

She had been right about the anonymous source. Her eyes widened and her mouth dropped open. He was the one who told Animal Control about Jasper. But something about the way he said it made her wonder if it was more than that. He made it seem as though they were on his side; as if they might actually be helping him.

She barely had time to think about that as he continued speaking. "You and that calf are going to pay," he gloated. "I don't care for meddlers."

To her horror, the man reached beside him and bent to pick up a gun she hadn't seen before. It wasn't the rifle from their encounter in the ocean. It was a pistol, and he was aiming it directly at KK.

"I heard something about dolphins never forgetting anything," he mused as he leveled the gun at her. All KK could do was swim, but the barrel of the pistol followed her movements. "I don't think that matters much if they're dead, though."

The pistol fired.

KK dove beneath the water, but she heard the bullet slamming into the water behind her, strangely muted and distorted by the liquid. If she hadn't ducked when she did, she would have been dead.

Yet again, she was stuck beneath the water with no safe way of resurfacing.

She heard another gunshot, and this time she saw the bullet hit and move through the water to her right. She was dead. He wouldn't keep missing with her pinned like this. But she couldn't let him kill Jasper or hurt anyone else. She wouldn't. She closed her eyes, trying to think of something, anything, she could do to avoid her inevitable fate.

The water distorted to her left, but it wasn't a bullet. There was too much water displacement for that. Then she felt something silky smooth brush against her skin for the briefest of seconds. Then, a garbled, muted, angry cry of pain, muffled by the water but still clearly audible, echoed from above.

A need to know what had happened overcame her self-preservation and she broke the surface. She gasped for air as she turned to look at the overhang, then blinked the water from her eyes, certain it had distorted her vision.

But no. Her eyes weren't wrong. The poacher was lying down on the metal overhang, screaming in pain as he aimed the pistol. But the gun was no longer pointing at KK. Instead, it was pointed at the bottlenose dolphin calf who was pinning the man's leg to the floor. Jasper had leaped from the water and onto the overhang to stop the poacher. He was clicking and whistling angrily as he thrashed, keeping the man in place.

"Jasper, back!" KK called in a panic. He was a sitting duck, and she couldn't let Jasper get shot for her.

The calf looked at her, then back at the poacher, then back to her. Just before the gun went off for the third time, Jasper wiggled and slid back into the water, and the bullet went harmlessly over him. He gracefully swam over and stopped right in front of her, placing himself between KK and the poacher.

Footsteps and yells came from the doorway toward the outdoor arena. The poacher looked, his face twisted into a snarl of loathing and anger.

"This isn't over," he spat, stumbling to his feet. He was favoring the leg Jasper hadn't sat on, but he was still glowering at the two of them. "You both are going to pay."

The sounds were still growing louder, and the man shot KK and Jasper one more withering glare, then ran away towards the back tank where she had first found him, limping as he did.

"KK!" Nikki gasped as she, Deborah, Tim, and Tony all appeared at the side of the tank, looking shocked and panicked.

"I'll go after him," Tim promised.

"Don't," KK panted, the adrenaline beginning to wear off now that the danger had passed. "Don't. He has a gun."

But Tim either ignored her or didn't hear her, and ran off despite the warning. Tony and Deborah hurried up to the overhang and helped KK clamber out. She lay there for a moment, still panting as the relief washed over her.

Tim appeared a moment later. "He ran out the side door," he informed them. "There was a car waiting for him. It peeled out before I could get the plates."

"It's fine," KK assured them, sitting up. "We're safe. That's all that matters right now."

"I managed to calm Jasper down," Tim said. "Except then he went ballistic. He ran off into the tube to this tank and didn't listen to any of my commands. A moment later, we heard the gunshots."

"He saved my life," KK whispered, bending over and stroking the dolphin, who was floating near the overhang, clicking worriedly. "Thanks, buddy."

Jasper leaned into her caresses, nuzzling her hand. He chittered at her in a way that unmistakably meant, I'll always look after you.

Chapter Fourteen

"Ladies and gentlemen, welcome to Marine World!" KK announced. The audience cheered and clapped as she hopped onto the fake rocks above the outdoor arena tank. "We've got a really special treat for you guys today. He's one of my best friends and the newest addition to the team. He's a little nervous, so everyone please give a warm welcome to Jasper!"

At his name, Jasper broke through the surface of the water. He jumped straight up, spinning midair as the audience cheered.

"This is Jasper's debut performance, and he's really excited to be here."

Jasper chattered and began tail-walking backwards before backflipping and landing back in the water. His tail slapped the surface, sending a wave crashing over the side of the tank and onto the first two rows. The kids sitting there screamed in delight before devolving into peels of laughter.

Standing about ten feet away from her, Tim grabbed a fish and lobbed it into the air for Jasper to catch, before having them do a series of backflips.

KK cracked a smile. After everything that had happened, it seemed a miracle that they had gotten here. But here they were, and everything was going better than she could have imagined.

After the poacher had run away and KK and the others were certain the danger had passed, they called the police. They had come, and took her at least mildly seriously when she presented the bruises on her head and neck from her skirmish with the poacher, and when she pointed to the bullets that had settled at the bottom of the tank. But they hadn't believed her when she had suggested that he might have some contacts or connections with Animal Control, telling her that she had probably been imagining it or that she was just being hysterical during a highly stressful situation. It had taken all of her willpower to keep her mouth shut when Officer Akamai had said that. But despite the dubiousness, Kremer had at least put out an APB now that KK was able to provide him with a good description.

Thankfully, after testing all the tanks, it seemed as though the poacher had only managed to pour bleach into one tank. They had drained it and scrubbed it clean with environmentally friendly cleaners. Now that the broken tank had finally been repaired, all their tanks were operational again, which was a massive relief.

Still, it was hard for KK not to worry about the poacher. She kept wondering if he would come back. She double and triple-checked all of the equipment, and had the locksmith come in to change all the locks, and had even switched out the wetsuits so he couldn't hide in plain sight anymore. But she was still worried he would find ways to cause trouble.

She pushed those fears from her head. Now wasn't the time to worry about it. This was Jasper's debut show, and her parents and all of her friends were here to watch and cheer her on. Pamela was sitting near the back, licking the filling from one of Uncle Senior malasada's off her fingers. Reese and Nikki were off to one side, cheering as Jasper did a series of swimming maneuvers below the surface of the water. Tony was near them, smiling up, but his eyes were fixed on KK, not the dolphin. Reese whispered something into Nikki's ear. Nikki glanced over at Tony, then at KK, then whispered something back to Reese, and the two women started giggling, though their laughter was drowned out by the applause. She had no idea what that was about, but she ignored it. She had more important things to concentrate on at the moment.

Jasper went through a series of solo tricks, much to the audience's delight. Jasper was loving it and hamming it up whenever possible.

"He's a natural, but he's still got a bit to learn," KK mused. "Thankfully, our resident twins, Carey and Corey, are here to help."

The other two dolphins swam in front of the tube, swimming for the surface and arcing through the water simultaneously to make their entrance. Jasper joined them, and the three of them bobbed up and down in unison, before doing alternating flips and backflips. It was remarkable how well the three of them worked together, especially considering how contentious the twins had been toward Jasper in the beginning. Out in the crowd, her parents were watching with undisguised amazement as she and Tim continued leading the dolphins through their moves. Her mother was beaming with pride, and her father was grinning, leaning forward in his seat, completely immersed in what was unfolding before him.

Off to one side, as she went through her monologue, KK's eyes landed on two unpleasantly familiar people in Animal Control uniforms. Pete and Jenna were standing off to one side, watching intently. Pete was wearing sunglasses, but the scowl he was giving made it obvious what he was thinking. Jenna was more inscrutable. KK's heart stuttered for the briefest moment as she regarded them. Then she forced herself to tear her gaze away from them. She couldn't worry about them, not in the middle of the show, and not when she had no reason to fear them.

"All right, everyone," KK continued. "Now who here isn't afraid of getting a little wet?"

Most of the hands went into the air. KK scanned the crowd before pointing at a girl in a bathing suit who was waving her hand energetically back and forth, stretching her arm to the limit in desperation to be seen. KK pointed to her.

"How would you feel about going for a little ride?" KK asked. The girl squealed audibly over the applause of the crowd.

Deborah led the girl up to the rocky overhang. Carey was already waiting patiently by the side of the rocks. She whistled politely and clicked hello to the little girl, who giggled excitedly as she petted the dolphin. Deborah muttered into the girl's ear a few instructions, then guided her onto the dolphin's back. Carey remained where she was until Deborah had mounted Corey next to her, and the twins and their riders began swimming around the tank. The little girl laughed and screamed in delight as they glided through the water. KK smiled fondly, remembering her first time riding a dolphin when she wasn't much younger than the girl.

Deborah and the girl dismounted, the girl a bit more clumsily, and the audience clapped as she teetered back to her seat.

It was time for the grand finale. KK's heart thundered, but more with excitement than fear. She knew what was about to happen. She glanced over at Tim to confirm he was ready, and he nodded.

"We're almost out of time but before we go, Tim over here has been working with Jasper on a special move," KK announced. "He thinks Jasper is ready to show it off to all of you lovely people, so let's see what they've been working on."

She took a few steps back. Tim waved to everyone, giving his quintessential influencer smolder. Then, grinning like a maniac, he ran forward and jumped into the water. The lights in the tank flickered out leaving only an inky blackness of waves against the glass. The crowd gasped in unison.

Over in the corner, Pete and Jenna jerked slightly but stayed where they were. Peggi was in the front row of the audience, phone in front of her face, her eyes wide with anticipation. There was a long minute where nothing happened above the dark water. Even the dolphins were underwater. Then, Jasper and Tim rose out of the water and the audience lost their minds.

The inner tank pulsed to life, emitting dazzling beams of gold and silver light as they illuminated Tim, who was balancing on Jasper's nose on one hand in a perfect one-handed handstand, legs high above his head. Not only that, Jasper was still swimming through the water while Tim stayed upside down. Tim waved to the audience with his free hand, many of whom whipped out their phones to record, while Peggi cheered louder than the rest of them, her face beaming with pride and affection even as she filmed.

It seemed impossible that this had been the same injured calf KK had met a handful of months ago. She doubted Jasper would do that trick for anyone but her or Tim, but seeing it vindicated everything she had done. Looking out in the crowd, her parents were slack-jawed. Pamela had stopped eating malasadas to gape in amazement. The Animal Control agents looked at one another, and then stalked away, leaving the arena.

Jasper and Tim did two laps around the tank, long enough for the audience to get their fill of photos and videos, while the twins followed behind them, jumping up in the air in tandem. Just as Tim's arm was starting to shake, Jasper dipped below the water, allowing Tim to reposition himself so he was on Jasper's back. Then Jasper led him to the edge of the rock overhang and Tim climbed off. He patted Jasper's head, then tossed him a fish, before waving to the audience and giving an ostentatious bow.

"All right, everyone," KK called over the roar of the crowd. "That's all we've got time for. Thank you so much for coming, and please know that our knowledgeable staff will stay around for a bit longer to answer any questions you might have. We hope you had a great time and that you got to learn something new."

The moment she stepped off the metal stairs, she was accosted by Reese, Pamela, Nikki, Tony, and her parents.

"That was amazing!" Nikki gushed, hugging her. "You didn't tell me you guys had done that much work."

"Told you Jasper would be a star," her dad said, grinning proudly. "That was incredible, honey."

"We're so proud of you," her mom beamed, her eyes shimmering with joy.

"Just don't forget to make sure they get some rest tonight," her father lectured. "And you should always mention the gift shop and individual dolphin rides at the end of the show. It's the best way to upsell—"

"Dad," KK moaned. "No business advice."

"I wasn't giving business advice," her dad protested. He paused, then turned to Katerina. "Was I?"

"You were," Katerina confirmed, smiling and giving Joseph a peck on the lips. "But that's okay, we like you anyway."

"That was incredible, KK," Tony grinned. "Knew you could do it." He nudged her in a way that was supposed to be playful but instead made her awkwardly stumble over her feet. "Great job," He added, clearing his throat and rubbing the back of his neck nervously.

Dizzy with excitement, KK grinned. She glanced over at Jasper, who was swimming close to them, watching the exchange through the tank. He saw her looking and chattered affectionately, doing backflips in the water. She knew what he was saying.

We did it.

Chapter Fifteen

"It looks so amazing," Reese gasped, eyes wide as saucers as she stepped into the finally-completed Sanctuary. "I can't believe it."

"Unglaublich," Pamela breathed, looking all around. "So schön."

KK knew enough German to understand: Incredible; so beautiful. And she had to agree. Like Reese, KK couldn't fully believe it, either. The final touches of furniture and decoration had finally completed the Sanctuary, and it was better than KK had ever imagined. The large, circular open area in the middle had the natural sunlight from the glass dome overhead shining down on it. The koi pond, filled with catfish and goldfish as well as koi, was off-set near a cozy sitting area with a bar and couches. Natural moss and stone walkways covered the ground.

Off to one side was a small but elegant garden with a waterfall that spilled into the koi pond. Hammocks were interspersed in various corners and nooks, giving it an almost exotic feel. It was absolutely stunning, and it was finally complete.

"Over here is the break area," KK gestured to the seating area in the center, as she gave Reese, Pamela, Nikki, and Tony the final tour. Tim and Deborah were off that day; she'd show it to them later. "And the hammocks are for anyone who needs a quick nap, or for me when I stay late. There's a kitchen over there to the right, which is where staff can take lunch now so you aren't eating over the tanks anymore—"

"That was one time!" Tony protested.

"The bar is fully stocked and is for anyone who wants to hang out after work," KK continued, nudging Tony playfully as she pretended to ignore him. "There are also some books and a TV and some consoles if people want to unwind with video games or kill some time."

"You're really going to make it difficult to make people want to work," Nikki muttered. "And that's coming from me."

"You did good," Tony said admiringly, looking all around. "Honestly, I didn't know what it was supposed to look like when you tried to explain it to me. But this is great. I can't wait to hide out in here when I'm trying to avoid work."

"Maybe don't tell your boss that's your plan until after you've implemented it," KK rolled her eyes. "Now this is going to be the first place I look."

"Oops."

"It really is incredible," Nikki gushed.

"I just wish the finishing touches hadn't taken so long," KK grumbled. "But it's done now. That's really all that matters." Her eyes lit up with excitement and her smile widened. "Speaking of done…"

She trotted happily over to where her cross-stitch sat on the oak coffee table resting in the center of the sitting area. She held it up triumphantly as the rest of the group crowded up to look at it.

"Oh, it looks great!" Nikki cried. "Look at the cute little guy."

Pamela leaned in, eyeing it critically. "You missed two stitches there," she said, pointing at the outstretched fin.

"That was intentional," KK admitted, smiling. "It's supposed to be Jasper. Granted, he's healed now, so it isn't a one-to-one, but I'm slow, so just go with it."

Pamela squinted, looking even closer. Then she let out a hmph of acknowledgment and nodded once. It was one of Pamela's highest compliments.

"I still can't believe how well Jasper is doing in the show," Tony remarked. "I mean, it was really impressive. And I never would have imagined the twins sharing the limelight with anyone, let alone letting Jasper take center stage."

"I wouldn't have believed it until I saw it, either," KK agreed. "I don't know what happened. It's pretty weird, but, hey, I'm not going to question it."

"He's a good guy," Tony mused. "I like him."

"Me too," KK agreed. "Which is why I'm thrilled that Rosie called me the other day to tell me Animal Control is going to be off my back for a bit."

"Really?" Reese's eyebrows shot up.

"Yup! Apparently, she worked her Rosie magic and went all bulldog on them. Started talking about abuse of power and all that fun stuff and they quieted down pretty quickly."

"I love that woman," Nikki sighed.

"You and I both," KK laughed. "She said it was probably only temporary. They'll start poking around again eventually. But, hey, she got them off our back for now, and just some time to breathe is really what we needed after everything."

"Just as long as she didn't make them a permanent enemy of Marine World," Reese warned.

"Well, if she did, we'll worry about that when it happens," KK assured her. "Which, considering everything we've gone through over the last few months, having a couple of grumpy Animal Control agents annoyed with us seems pretty inconsequential."

"So there really hasn't been any sign of the poachers since he tried to shoot you?" Pamela asked.

"Nothing," KK confirmed. "No sabotage, no threats, no strangers lurking around or anything like that. It's been three months and I haven't heard a peep."

The first month, she'd been entirely on edge, waiting for a dark figure to follow her home or for someone lurking in the shadows to pull a gun on her, or for her to come in one morning to find all the tanks devoid of water, the dolphins dead or stolen. It had seemed like an inevitability. But there had been nothing. She hadn't even heard of any poaching or dead animals washing ashore. It seemed like the danger was over. She supposed she had scared off the poachers for good.

"Well that's a relief," Tony breathed. "You've got enough to worry about without having to add homicidal poachers to the list."

The rest murmured their agreements. Pamela muttered something under her breath in German that KK didn't catch.

"It's over with," KK sighed. "That's all that matters. Now I can worry about more important things."

"Like your next cross-stitch pattern," Pamela chimed in.

"That's true." Tony reached over and grabbed her bag, holding it out for her. "Any ideas on what you'll do next?"

"Actually, yes!" KK proclaimed. She opened the bag and began rummaging through it. "I found this really cute pattern of a beach online and I printed it out. I think it's in here somewhere...Ah! There we go."

She fished out a folded sheet and noticed a piece of paper stuck to it. She had forgotten that the poacher's notes were still in her bag. Something had kept her from throwing them away; a gut feeling, perhaps, that despite what she told the others, this wasn't really over.

Pamela called out, "Did you find it?" KK nodded and stuffed the notes back into her bag. She started back to the group, but when she opened the paper with the pattern, ready to show everyone, the smile on her face froze before slowly sliding off.

"What is it?" Tony asked.

She didn't answer, just stared at the piece of paper in disbelief as worry crept over her. It wasn't her cross-stitch pattern, that was for sure. In an unpleasantly familiar scrawl were the words:

Don't forget to change your locks.

"KK?" Nikki asked in a panic. KK looked up to see all her friends staring at her with concern.

She forced a smile and crumbled the sheet of paper in her hand. A shiver ran down her spine before she shoved it back into her bag and headed toward her friends, a brighter smile on her face, "Silly me, I forgot to print it out."

For now, she wanted to celebrate with her friends.

There was plenty of time later for her to continue digging into the man who left these mysterious messages and had shot at her twice.

Plenty of time to hunt him and his friends down.
Plenty of time for her to—
...finally get justice.

Don't be shy...

Dear Cozy Readers,

Thank you for reading my book! I would greatly appreciate hearing from each and every one of you. My email is below.

Feel free to reach out to me anytime to share your thoughts on a series, a book, or a character that you found particularly enjoyable (or maybe not so enjoyable!).

And hey, if you have any fantastic story ideas, don't hesitate to let me know. I might take a shot at it.

Remember, I'm always here for you if you want to connect!

I respond to every email that comes my way from my cozy fans!

Toodles!

~Peyton Stone

PeytonStone.com (need a new mug with another book?)

Email: hello@peytonstone.com ← say hi!

Made in the USA
Columbia, SC
12 June 2024